WINDWILL TOWN

BOOK 1

THE SEDUCTION

WRITTEN BY

CHRISTOPHER ERIC OUTRIDGE (CEO)

THIS BOOK IS A WORK OF FICTION.

PHOTO CREATED BY CRAIG FERRENCE

STREET SIGN CREATED BY DAN DIANA
AND CRAIG FERRENCE

MODEL: BRIGITTE ARREDONDO

ISBN: 978-0-6151-6906-4

THIS BOOK IS DEDICATED TO

MY BELOVED FAMILY,

WHO I LOVE MORE THAN ANY

WORDS OR EMOTIONS CAN DESCRIBE.

THANK YOU FOR ALWAYS BEING THERE

FOR ME.

I ALSO WANT TO THANK AND DEDICATE

THIS BOOK TO ALL MY FRIENDS WHO

HAVE ALSO SUPPORTED ME

THROUGHOUT MY CAREER.

THANK YOU TO EVERYONE!!!!!!

PROLOGUE

The morning sun shines even though it is a cold, gloomy day. Dark clouds cover the sun, not allowing its beams to shine on the city beneath it. Typical of this city, even in the day it never gets any sunlight.

Windwill Town, USA.

A very old city that once was run by farmers and cow herders, is now governed by whores, criminals and pimps. The lands in this city used to provide nutrients and soils for crops and livestock. However, since industrialization, the only thing that these lands provide is just another place for the unlawful to hide away. There are cops in this town, but the number of robbers, murderers, rapists, pimps, whores and just all around scum bags out number the law about 20 to 1. Not to mention the fact that the cops in town are all, for the most part, crooked cops who will more likely cover up a crime than stop one for occurring.

You can't make any arrests if you can't catch anybody.

The streets in this town are dirty and inhabited by stray animals and homeless people, who have no other place to go but cardboard boxes in alleys. Since the sun has risen, there aren't any prostitutes out and most of the strip clubs, bars and penthouses are closed for business. Anyone who is out of their beds right now are the very few people who still give a damn, the people who have honest jobs or responsibilities that they have to accomplish before the lights go out and everything turns to shit.

If you are not amongst those people, then you are amongst the very few rich bastards who are out of their beds, delegating and ordering around the hopeless saps who work for you.

Maybe this place didn't change from what it was several decades ago. There are still farmers, only now instead of producing crops they produce machinery, drugs, alcohol and hookers. There are also still ranchers, except their livestock has changed from large fat cows to large fat middle aged men who are either too lazy, too poor or too stupid to do anything else other than manual labor.

Windwill Town, USA, a once fruitful and prosperous town has wasted away to nothing. The lives of its inhabitants has changed with the town; people with ambitions and goals that have deteriorated to lost hopes and forgotten dreams.

CHAPTER 1

"Move that crate kid, you're lagging behind!!!!"

Andy Combs can hear his boss yelling at him from across the room. The boss has to be yelling at him, everything is always Andy's fault. Even if it isn't his shift, it has to always be Andy's fault.

Another crate is lifted onto the dolly so that the two other warehouse workers can carry its contents into the loading bay. Each crate is filled with dozens of rusted or damaged metal equipment, which is set to be shipped over to the Windwill Town Recycling Plant later that afternoon. Upon arrival at the Recycling Plant, these pieces of equipment will be refurbished, reconstructed and then sent back into economic circulation as brand spankin new used products.

Located in the outskirts of Windwill Town, Metal Parts Depot is the leading company responsible for the collection, housing and packaging of all metal things that are useless to others.

Every morning, the warehouse workers at Metal Parts Depot have to sort through each piece of scrap metal, pack up the crates with the metal, label the crates, carry the crates onto the dolly, drive the dolly to the truck, unload the dollies and then send the truck onto its merry way to the Windwill Town Recycling Plant. They do this all morning until they punch their time cards in at 4 in the afternoon. At that point, the afternoon shift will come in and do the same exact thing all afternoon and night long.

Pretty decent work for only 5.75 an hour.

Half the workers don't really understand how little they are being paid, since most of them are illegal immigrants who believe that 5.75 an hour can make them kings in the United States.

Andy knows that 5.75 an hour can't make him a king; it can't even qualify him as the court jester. However, he still continues to work here, lifting and labeling crates while straining and mangling his back.

Every morning for seven days a week, Andy works hard at the Depot. Andy will keep working hard just because this is one of the only jobs he can find that didn't involve selling anything, or anyone, illegal.

The workers place crate number 25 onto dolly number 5.

Andy can feel a sharp pain in his back, which only hurts more as the day goes by. He never had back problems until he started working for this company four years ago. A 24 year old young man with the back of an 80 year old can't be good.

Without a lunch break, Andy and the other workers work for several more hours. The snotty, arrogant and rich boss screams at him and everyone else in the warehouse, urges them to move faster and pack more into the crates.

"Everyone ounce of spaces in each box must be used." He orders, "Crates cost money!!!!!"

At the end of the day, Andy exhaustingly punches his timecard into the machine to clock himself out. He slowly walks out of the warehouse and heads towards the train station to continue his day.

<C>   <E>   <O>

Andy walks down into the subway station and over to a food cart that is set up by the stairwell. The brick and stone walls of the terminal are covered with graffiti and damaged advertisements. The smell of urine and sewage water is so strong that it has become a permanent aroma in this atmosphere. Also, simply due to the mentality of the city, there is a good amount of litter soiling the floors of the station.

From the looks of the subway, one will instantly realize that it isn't regularly or properly maintained. Subway workers and owners probably don't give a damn about the condition of the stations; nobody important ever has to ride on the subways in Windwill Town anyway. However, in their defense, there are just too many people messing it up too often for anybody to notice that it is actually being cleaned.

It is time for lunch; a 75 cent candy bar and a $1.50 bottle of soda. Not an improvement over the bagel and orange juice he had for breakfast eight hours ago at the warehouse, but he has to eat something fast and quick. This small window of time while waiting for the train is probably the only time he will have to eat for the rest of the day. As soon as he hands his money to the man behind the counter, the train pulls into the station.

The doors open and a swarm of passengers leave the train. Andy runs for the train, managing to get into a car before the door closes. He finds a seat close to the door and sits down.

Oh, does it feel good to sit down and relax.

Once settled, he reaches for his candy bar and soda so that he can eat. The candy bar is present, but the soda is nowhere to be found. As the train car drives off, he notices that his soda bottle laying on the platform outside of the train, partially opened and spilling out soda onto the concrete.

He must have dropped it while running to the train.

A homeless man triumphantly picks up the bottle from the dirty floor and drinks it happily. Andy turns away from the window with great sadness as the homeless man dances and waves the soda bottle in the air with glee.

Another $1.50 donation to the homeless.

Moore's Bar and Grill is a very popular restaurant in Windwill Town. The dinner area is very well maintained; all of the seat cushions are well kept and very comfortable and each table is cleaned after each use. The floors are made of hard wood, just like the large bar located in the center of the facility. The food is also very delicious, and the selection includes everything from burgers and French fries to specialty meals and vegetarian dishes. Very few places in Windwill Town are clean, tidy and affordable, so if you are looking for a sanitary and cheap restaurant to dine in, Moore's Bar and Grill is most likely where you will end up.

Unfortunately, it isn't the best place to work.

The dining room area is comfortable and inviting, but the kitchen area is hostile and degrading to all employees. Imagine a really small sweatshop filled with cooking equipment and a dishwashing station. The workers are all quiet, honest people who are working hard just to get some cash to survive in this world. Their managers are tyrants, who really don't care about anything but the money that comes out of the registers at closing.

The crew often go long hours without and a break, and when they do get a break, they aren't allowed to eat the food that they make without paying the full price of what they are ordering.

The term "employee discount" doesn't exist in Windwill Town, and while we are on the subject, it is safe to say that the term "overtime" is also nonexistent.

Why is it that every business in Windwill Town treats their workers like crap?

This is Andy's second job, a late night dishwasher at Moore's Bar and Grill. After a hard and grueling day of moving and lifting boxes, Andy comes to Moore's Bar and Grill to wash other people's dishes and be disrespected by his managers and some of his co workers. So during the day, the kitchen staff dirty the dishes, and at closing, they are shoved off to Andy so that he can clean them.

While Andy is cleaning all the dishes, the rest of the kitchen crew has to clean and stock their stations and mop the kitchen and dining room floors. They do this while hungry since none of them are allowed to eat any of the food that they are throwing away. The managers count up their inventory and sales and when they finish this simple task, they sit back and watch while everyone else works for the rest of the night.

If you're not a manager, you won't get any respect working at Moore's Bar and Grill. Except of course, and this isn't even respect, you are a vulnerable and attractive waitress who is forced into sex with one or all of the managers in order to keep your job. Even now, Andy can see out of the corner of his eye the 47 year old general manager guiding one of the 19 year old waitresses into the office and locking the door behind her.

She needs a raise in order to stay in college.

In reality, Andy actually doesn't mind washing dishes at all much. After a long morning of moving scrap metal and crates, washing dishes becomes a very relaxing and simple task. He is still on his feet all night during his shift at Moore's Bar and Grill, but at least he doesn't have to do any heavy lifting.

Andy finishes up the first batch dishes. He has been washing for about an hour and a half. The 19 year old girl left the office about twenty minutes ago, her arms folded across her chest and her head hanging low. She is trying not to cry, heading up to the front counter in order to continue to serve guests. The manager steps out of the office next, rubbing his crotch and slapping the girl's ass, while she tries to go back to work and pretend that everything is still the same.

What else could she do, she needs the money for college.

That is what it is like in Windwill Town; you can't get anywhere if you don't sell yourself to someone or pay someone off in order to get there. As depressing as this sounds, most people end up being forced into or willing walking down one of these roads.

Only a few decide to struggle.

Andy has decided to struggle.

After washing two more rounds of dishes, Andy cleans the sink and then his back area. After that, Andy has to put away the new shipment of food and clean the bathrooms. Only two more hours left, and then Andy can go home.

<C>   <E>   <O>

It is 1:30 am when Andy walks through the door of the apartment building project where his apartment resides. Andy lives in Southmount, one of the forgotten slums of Windwill Town. Aside from the frequent muggings and the random kidnappings, nothing really happens around here because no one cares enough to recognize that this slum exists. He lives mostly with people like himself; people who either can't afford to live any place else, or people who still have hope of having something better.

Everyone else living in the building are gang members, prostitutes and strippers. The gang members are here because the people in the area can be easily robbed or otherwise taken advantage of. The prostitutes and strippers are here because their work places, (clubs as well as street corners), are all within a ten minute walk away from the building.

Andy walks his normal route home; the route that takes him the furthest away from the muggers' usual hideouts. Andy lives on the fifth and top floor of the building, which means that his chances of being robbed are greater than most since he has the longest travel time to his apartment. Fortunately for Andy, most of the gang members understand the fact that he is extremely broke and think that robbing him is useless.

So instead of robbing and battering him, they just batter him and leave him in the hallway with his already empty wallet still in his pocket.

In one piece, he reaches his apartment on the fifth floor. Still watching his back, He quickly opens his door and enters his home. Andy closes the door slowly and leans against it for a few minutes, resting his body after a very long day's work.

Andy's studio apartment is small and clean despite the condition of some of the walls. The apartment only has three rooms; a kitchen, a living room and a bathroom. The pipes in the kitchen are leaking water and are rusted due to neglect by the landlord. There is very little cooking equipment in the kitchen and very little food in the refrigerator. Other than that, and the fact that the cabinets need some serious fixing, the kitchen isn't in bad condition at all.

He sleeps on the couch in his living room, right next to his small television set that barely works and has no cable. He has a night table next to his couch, where his alarm clock and phone sit. There is a closet next to the door where all of Andy's clothes and shoes are kept. The living room is the cleanest place in the studio, although the walls can use a new paint job and the carpets are long overdue to be replaced with new ones.

The bathroom is smallest room in the apartment. There is mildew growing between the tiles in the shower and around the toilet, and despite Andy's best efforts to clean it, the mildew doesn't seem to want to go away. Sometimes the hot water runs cold and more often, the water just won't run at all.

Finally gathering the strength to move, Andy walks into his living room and sits down on his couch. He once again takes a moment to relax, his back finding comfort in the couch cushions. He turns to his night table and notices that there is a small red light flashing on his home phone. The counter on the phone tells him that he has 2 voice mail messages saved on the machine. Leaning forward to reach the phone, Andy presses the message button and hears his voice mail messages play out.

"Hello, this is Mr. Hoyt calling for Mr. Andy Combs. We have received your story and after careful review we have decided not to publish your work. We don't feel that your story is the right project that our company should focus on. We are sorry and wish you good luck in the future."

Andy signs in disappointment, holding his face in his hands. Andy's dream is to one day be a writer. He writes mostly dramas as well as poetry. Whenever Andy has the money, which isn't often at all, Andy mails out his stories hoping to one day be picked up by a publisher. His work has always been shot down though, and although it depresses him each time, he has gotten used to the feeling.

The second message plays.

"Hey Andy it's Tony. Where have you been man? I haven't seen you in ages. Listen Andy, when you get a chance give me a call. We have to hang out sometime. I'm off on Thursday, so if you are not doing anything let me know. Call me back."

The answering machine informs Andy that he has played all of his messages. Andy slumps back on his couch. Tony is right, it has been a while since he has been out with a friend, or anyone for that matter. Andy needs to work, he needs the....

The sound of his phone ringing, startles Andy from his thoughts. No one ever calls him this late. Andy remains on the couch, too tired to pick up the phone. The answering machine picks up the call and records the message. Andy can hear the message play.

"Hi Andy, its me, Amy." A woman says. She sounds very upset, almost as if she is about to cry. "I guess you're still at work. Andy, please give me a call whenever you get home, it doesn't matter how late it is. Please call me. I miss you." Amy hangs up the phone.

Andy remains immobile and silent. Amy is Andy's girlfriend. He loves her with all of his heart and hopes to one day marry her. They have been together since college and even when Andy had to drop out because he didn't have the money to pay for classes, Amy didn't leave his side. Amy and Andy have a wonderful relationship that is built on purity, trust and true love.

He hasn't seen her or spoken to her in three months.

Andy loves Amy and he knows that Amy loves him, but he can't get himself to believe that he deserves to have such a great woman like her. It hurts him to know that he isn't in any position to provide for her and take care of her the way he should be. Andy believes that Amy can do so much better than him, and she deserves to have all the things that every man in the world other than Andy can provide for her.

Andy wants to call her, but he can't get himself to pick up the phone.

He lays down in his couch, the exhaustion finally getting to him His eyes slowly begin to close and soon he falls fast asleep. Tomorrow morning, his day will start all over again, and nothing will get better.

That is a day in the life of Andy Combs in Windwill Town, USA.

CHAPTER 2

Andy wakes up bright and early in the morning and heads into the shower. Andy has always found showering to be relaxing, perhaps one of the most relaxing experiences of his life. The warm water makes his back feel a lot better after several long hours of working.

He finishes his shower and gets dressed for work at the warehouse. Andy goes to his kitchen and has some cereal for breakfast. He savors every bite of his cereal because it will probably be his only real meal until he gets home tomorrow morning.

Andy is now ready to go to work. He packs his restaurant uniform in his bag so that he can change when he gets to Moore's Bar and Grill. Andy sneaks out of his apartment, trying not to be noticed by anyone.

"Hey Hair Comb, get your ass over here."

So much for not getting noticed.

That guttural and raspy voice belongs to Andy's landlord, Mr. McGuckin. With every morning that passes, Andy hopes that he will leave his apartment without seeing Mr. McGuckin, and 5 out of 7 random mornings, he fails.

Mr. McGuckin is a fat, greasy, cigar smoking, hairy Irish man who smells like a raw sewage dump and looks like one too. Today he looks particularly unkept, wearing a yellow stained white t-shirt and soiled white underwear. His hair is also dirty, uncombed and greasy. He comes stomping out of his dirty apartment, which just happens to be next door to Andy's apartment, just as Andy walks out of his door.

Andy stops in the hallway and gives Mr.McGuckin a smile. He is very tired and in a lot of pain and on top of that, he hates Mr. McGuckin more than anything in the world. Andy's smile is so forced that it is coming out kicking and screaming.

"Where is my rent Hair Comb?" Mr. McGuckin growls as he blows a puff of smoke into Andy's face. Mr. McGuckin calls Andy "Hair Comb" because Andy has an average slim figure and his last name is Combs. How original.

"Mr. McGuckin I...." Andy begins too say.

"The rent should be in my hands Hair Comb." Mr. McGuckin grunts.

"I just need to get my paycheck from the warehouse and...." Andy begins to explain.

"How much money do you have in your pockets?" Mr. McGuckin asks.

Mr. McGuckin lounges forward and grabs Andy. He pushes his hands into Andy's pockets and pulls out Andy's wallet. Andy does nothing to stop the man as he looks through the wallet. He finds five dollars and a picture of Amy. Mr. McGuckin takes the picture and the money and throws the wallet down to the ground.

"I'll take this as a down payment." McGunkin grins as he puts the five dollars in his pocket.

"Sir I need that in order to eat lunch today." Andy informs while picking up his wallet.

"And I need to eat too Hair Comb." McGunkin yells, eyeing the picture of Amy, "I'll be accepting the rest of my rent next week in full."

"Yes sir." Andy gives in.

"Good." McGunkin says, licking his lips while looking at the picture of Amy, "Hey Andy, you should bring this hottie to my apartment one night. I'm willingly to lower your rent by a few dollars in exchange for sexual servicing."

McGunkin licks the picture with his unwashed tongue and sticks it in his pants. McGunkin walks into his apartment and closes the door.

Andy collects himself and goes to work. He leaves without his picture of Amy to comfort him and his five dollars to feed him.

<C>   <E>   <O>

Andy runs onto the train once again. This time, he doesn't drop his soda or candy bar, but the only reason why is because he didn't have the money to buy them.

The homeless man at the train station is very upset by this lack of money, and decides to express his dissatisfaction by spitting and cursing at Andy.

Andy is sitting on the train, and yes dear readers, he is still very tired. All day at work, he had trouble keeping his eyes open. As usual, it feels so relaxing to finally be able to sit down. Andy allows himself to get lost in relaxation, his eyelids closing and his thoughts drifting away.

"Hey Andy." someone says, "If I knew you took this train, I would leave my apartment early everyday."

Andy wakes up, startled by the person who is talking to him. His vision clears as he sees his best friend Tony Cruz sitting down next to him. Tony is an attractively built Spanish guy at 24 years of age. He is a very handsome man with long black hair and seductive green eyes. Andy gives Tony a weak smile.

"I'm sorry I woke you up." Tony politely says, "It's just that I haven't seen my best friend in a long time and I'm concerned. How have you been?"

"Good." Andy replies, clearly hiding his exhaustion.

"Lair." Tony says, "Listen, I'm off from work tomorrow and you really need to go out and have some fun. I want to take you out."

"I have to work tomorrow." Andy says, "I really need the money."

"But you also need to be healthy Andy." Tony explains, "Look at you, you are exhausted and in pain. You can't keep going on like this."

"I can't call out." Andy insists, "They may fire me."

"Then after work tomorrow I'm taking you out." Tony continues, "It will be my treat."

"You don't have to do that." Andy says.

"Yes I do." Tony says, "You're coming out with me tomorrow night and you are going to have a good time. Where is your night job?"

"At 50th and Anderson Lane." Andy says, "Moore's Bar and Grill."

"I'll be there at 1 am to pick you up." Tony says, "And don't try to get out of this. I won't take no for an answer."

The train stops at 30th Street which is Tony's stop. Tony stands up from his seat and shakes Andy's hand. "One more thing Andy." Tony says, "Call Amy. She really misses you." Tony heads off the train and it speeds away from the station.

Andy really misses Amy too.

<C>   <E>   <O>

Pierre's Diner is a 24 hour diner that serves a variety of different dishes for breakfast, lunch and dinner in Windwill Town. The building is located in a commercial part of town known as Loften, with a well maintained and inviting 80's like atmosphere to it.

But like all jobs in Windwill Town, working at Pierre's Diner isn't that pleasant. It is more pleasant than most, but it does have its hardships. The owner, Pierre Lyons, is a pervert and a sadist. He only hires female waitresses and definitely has them all work very hard (in the bedroom), in order to get a raise and keep their jobs. The only reason why he gets away with it is because Pierre is a rather young looking and very handsome French man at only thirty years of age. Also, most of the waitresses in the diner are whores, or women who just can't resist his amazing charm and provocative accent, or they are desperate and can't afford to lose their jobs. Pierre has slept with his entire waitressing staff since he opened several years ago.

Except for one.

Amy Swanson.

Amy is 22 years old, and like most well mannered individuals of Windwill Town, she is trying to get by and afford college and housing. Amy is a naturally beautiful woman with long brown hair and sexy black eyes. She has a good body and is very attractive. Unlike most of the women in Windwill Town, she dresses comfortably and casually. Amy doesn't use make up and is pretty much your "girl next door" type.

She isn't a whore, and she would rather be broke than trade sex for money. She has gotten raises during her year and a half long job at the restaurant, even though she has never had sex with

Pierre. Pierre has this insatiable infatuation towards the one waitress that he has never touched, and he keeps her around in hopes that he will have sex with her one day. He absolutely can't fire her or have her quit until he has fucked her.

She does feel uncomfortable working at the diner, knowing that everynight Pierre is fantasizing about ripping her clothes off and taking advantage of her against any random wall in the diner. There are also times when she feels that he is really going to do it. However, Amy will continue to work here as long as she still has the job because she really does need the money.

Plus, if she were to go some where else, they will actually force her against the wall and rape her.

That's what goes on in Windwill Town.

Amy places a tray of food on the table of a group of Truckers. They have ordered burgers and fries and are regular customers at the diner. Amy thinks that the only reason why they come in is because all the waitresses are very attractive young females who they can drool over everynight. Not to mention the fact that a pervert can catch a feel on a young waitress whenever they please without any consequence.

Why you ask? Well, remember what was said about sexual harassment earlier?

That's why.

Amy shudders when the man she has named Green Hat Trucker (for some reason this man always wears the same worn out green hat) grabs her ass. Amy shivers and then gives Green Hat Trucker an uneasy smile. This is the third time this week this man has grabbed her ass. Last week, he even wrote down his phone number on the check for her to have.

Green Hat Trucker licks his lips at Amy as she walks away. Amy really hates getting violated by customers, but she really can't do anything about it, not when living in Windwill Town. All Amy can do is constantly remind herself that it can be a lot worse.

Amy goes to the back to retrieve another tray of food when she feels her cell phone go off. It startles Amy at first, but she reaches for her phone, wondering why anyone would be calling her at 2 in the morning.

Amy sees Andy's name on her screen and she feels instantly overjoyed.

Amy loves Andy with all of her heart and soul. She met him in college and instantly fell in love with him, realizing that he is different from all other guys in Windwill Town. All of Amy's other boyfriends were only looking for sex, and were angry when Amy didn't reciprocate. One in particular raped her after their high school senior prom. After that incident, Amy didn't date again until she met Andy.

Andy helped her get over the trauma of getting raped and became one of the only people on Earth who can make her smile. Having met Andy is a great reward for living a life of seclusion and manipulation, and she always does everything in her power to make Andy happy.

Having not heard from Andy in so long hurts Amy a great deal. She spends everyday hoping that he is okay and that she can see him again soon. He told her that he has to work and organize the mess that his life is and then he will come back to her. She knows that he loves her, Amy just hopes that Andy doesn't forget the fact that she loves him as well.

And she always will.

Amy goes to answer her phone, forgetting the fact that she is at work. Before she can answer the call, Pierre grabs her wrist and takes the phone from her. She turns toward Pierre, who is holding her phone in the air to mock her. He slowly lets go of her wrist, allowing his hand to longingly drag down her arm.

"Is this an important call Amy that can't wait until you get off from work?" Pierre asks.

He dangles the phone above Amy, expecting her to jump up and down to try and get her phone back. Pierre likes being in a dominant position over Amy, so Amy tries to give him the least amount of satisfaction as she possibly can. She doesn't, and will not try to, get her phone back in this fashion.

"No sir." Amy says, "It isn't."

"So it looks like we are going to forget about our boyfriends and get back to work aren't we?" Pierre tells her while grinning and smiling down at Amy like a vulture.

"Yes." Amy says.

"Very good." Pierre says softly and seductively to her.

Pierre slowly lowers his arms and brings them to Amy's waist. He slides his hands on to her waist, slipping his thumbs underneath her shirt to touch Amy's skin. Amy can feel herself shivering as Pierre pulls her close to him.

"You know Amy." Pierre whispers, "A girl like you shouldn't be tied down to one man. You should be available to mingle and experience a new touch every now and then."

"I love him." Amy quickly and uneasily replies as Pierre's hands slides onto her hips, "I don't want anyone else."

Even though she is over having been raped, she still feels very uneasy when it a strange man is touching her. Just as always though, she thinks to herself that it can be allot worse.

"It's just a suggestion." Pierre whispers, slowly gliding his hands off of her and pocketing her phone, "I'll hold onto your phone until the end of your shift. When you're ready, you can go into my pants and get it."

Amy doesn't respond to him, her demeanor remaining strong in order to not show Pierre any satisfaction. Pierre acknowledges Amy's strength, but smirks anyway since he is in possession of her cell phone. Pierre rubs her cheek softly, his grin still plastered on his face. Without another word, he walks away with her cell phone in his pocket. Amy watches him go, mad at him for stealing her phone but trying her best to hide it.

Amy grabs her next tray of food and continues to do her job.

CHAPTER 3

The next day, just as Tony promised, he arrives at Moore's Bar and Grill at 1 am in order to pick Andy up from work. Andy, as usual, leaves work exhausted and wanting to go home, but Tony doesn't want to hear it. He leads Andy straight to the train station and onto the train so that they can go to the strip club.

And on the train, Andy continues his fight to go home.

"I really shouldn't be doing this." Andy says, "I have to work tomorrow. I should be getting some sleep."

"Just an hour at the club won't hurt you." Tony replies, "And anyway, you need this. You have to have some fun in your life while you're still young."

"I really should go home." Andy insists.

"You are not going home until you get at least one lap dance." Tony excitedly replies, "The club is just a twenty minute walk away from your apartment building. We'll have fun for an hour and you'll be home before you know it."

Andy sighs and then becomes silent for a second, finally giving up on the idea of going home. "I called Amy last night." Andy quietly says, "She didn't answer her phone."

"Well what time did you call her?" Tony asks.

"2 in the morning." Andy answers, feeling very depressed.

"She was probably sleeping." Tony reasons, "Or maybe she was at work. She works late sometimes too you know. The diner is 24 hours."

"She would have called me back then." Andy says.

"Alright Andy stop it now." Tony declares, "Amy loves you unconditionally and you know that."

"Amy deserves better than me." Andy replies, "Maybe she has finally realized that…."

Tony grabs Andy by the shoulders and looks him in the eye. "Amy loves you." Tony declares, "Listen, you and Amy need to see each other again. On your next day off, you will go out on a date with Amy."

"I can't afford to take her anywhere." Andy says.

"I'll give you the money to take her someplace nice." Tony replies, "You will accept it and you will have a great time."

"I can't spend your money." Andy says, "You need to survive."

"And so do you." Tony replies, "Grant it, I'm not a millionaire but you are a friend of mine and I can't see you so depressed like this. You will have a good time tonight, and you will go out with Amy and have a good time with her."

"I can't accept your offer." Andy says.

"You will accept my offer." Tony sternly demands, "You have no choice. When is your next day off?"

Andy gives up once again. "I'm off on Sunday." He answers.

"Then Sunday it is." Tony calls out in excitement, "I'll call Amy tomorrow and make arrangements. I'll make it happen, I promise."

The train stops at the Old Town Road station in Southmount. Tony and Andy get off the train and head towards the strip club.

<C>   <E>   <O>

Fantasia's Surrender is one of Windwill Town's hottest strip clubs. The owners, who consist of an elite team of the town's richest pimps and gangsters, really know how to do business. Fantasia's Surrender is more than just a strip club, it is a sexual palace of pleasure. This is a place where you can buy sex with certain strippers at very high prices, and you can also purchase plenty of illegal substances and alcohol fresh from the counter.

Oh, and they sell condoms too.

Fantasia's Surrender only hires the most beautiful and sultry women who apply, and surprisingly they are all of age. Every woman who dances or waitresses in this club is top notch. They offer a VIP room, private party rooms, lap dance stations and the ever popular but exclusive and secretive, F-Room (use your imagination on this one). And on top of all this, the club is 100% nudity all the time.

Well, except for one dancer, the club's main attraction. You'll meet her in about three pages from now.

Basically, every man who steps into Fantasia's Surrender will leave sexually satisfied and very broke if they don't control themselves accordingly.

So why isn't Andy having as much fun as everyone else is?

Tony and Andy entered the club about forty minutes ago and found seats two rows away from the main stage. Tony buys Andy and himself a soda and they start watching the women dance on the stage.

Andy isn't really into whorish and aggressive women. He will even admit that they scare him from time to time. One particular woman on stage is this very attractive blonde, who had to be a 36D with long slender legs and a toned body. The woman must be some type of gymnast or even a contortion artist, because this woman bends and moves her body in ways that Andy doesn't think is biologically possible.

Several women came by to offer Tony and Andy a lap dance during the hour that they have been in the club. Tony steers them to Andy, and Andy turns them all down. Andy finds it incredible that so many women have approached him so quickly. They truly are relentless in this place.

"Come on man relax and have some fun." Tony says, "Look at that one over there? Where are you going to find another girl like that who is willing to be all over you?"

Andy looks in the direction where Tony is pointing. The woman has light brown hair and green eyes and has a very nice Puerto Rican figure. She is wearing a really short skirt with a bra that looks like it is made out of dental floss. She is about to take the stage and dance for the crowd.

"If she asks you for a lap dance and you are accepting it." Tony says.

"I really shouldn't be here." Andy sighs, "Isn't this considered cheating?"

"No, it is considered having fun." Tony says, "Amy won't mind that you are here. You're just looking."

"But if I get a lap dance, I'm touching." Andy reasons.

"No, they are touching you." Tony says, "You are still just watching."

There is a pause.

"This is wrong, I can't...." Andy breaks the silence.

"What can't you do honey?" a woman asks, sitting herself on Andy's lap. Andy looks up at the woman, who starts running her hands through his hair. This woman has long, blonde hair with pink streaks in it. She is about 5.5, with a perfectly round ass and 36C bra size that is all natural. Her skin is soft and flawless and her shapely and defined figure shows that she spends time in the gym. She has full moist lips and quite possibly the sexiest gray eyes Andy has ever seen. She swings herself onto Andy's lap and wraps her arms around his neck.

"You look exhausted honey." The woman asks, straddling Andy while wearing nothing but a thong and a bra, "Can I be the one to wear you out?" The woman nods her head towards the F-Room and licks her lips while sliding her hands up Andy's chest.

"I have a girlfriend." Andy responds quickly, as she starts unbuttoning his shirt.

"I don't care." The woman whispers, "She can join us if she wants." The woman leans in forward to kiss Andy. Tony watches anxiously, waiting for Andy's reaction.

Before her lips can reach his, Andy pulls her off of him as if he is removing his bare hands from a steaming hot plate. The woman looks down at him in surprise, catching herself before she falls off of his lap. Tony buries his head in his hands in embarrassment.

"Oh god, oh god...." Andy frantically exclaims, "We can't do this. It is so wrong, I don't even know you."

He begins to brush the woman off of his lap. She jumps off of him willingly, eyeing him with a look of mockery and disgust.

The woman places her hands on her hips and laughs. "It's okay honey." The woman mocks Andy, "You wouldn't have been able to satisfy me anyway." The woman leaves, moving two tables over and placing herself on the lap of some 30 year old guy dressed in a pinstriped suit. After two minutes, they were heading for the F-Room.

"Oh god, oh god." Andy tells Tony, "Please don't tell Amy. I can't believe I did that."

"What did you do?" Tony asks in disappointment.

"She was all over me." Andy declares in protest, "What else could I have done? Please don't tell Amy."

"I won't tell Amy." Tony says, "I won't tell anyone."

"Look I'm sorry, but this really isn't for me." Andy says with a sign, "These girls are...sinister. They are vultures, scavengers."

"Alright let's go." Tony says in disappointment, "Next time I'll take you to a toy store."

The dancers leave the stage and the audience cheers and begs for an encore. Tony and Andy start to clean up their area to leave. They are just about to get out of their seats when the lights in the club unexpectedly go out and the entire room goes completely dark.

"Hello gentlemen, I hope all of you are having the most arousing time of your life." An unknown man over a loudspeaker call outs, "Now that your blood is freshly racing through your veins, you have all become the perfect meal for our star attraction."

Everyone in the club looks around in confusion, mesmerized by an eerie and gothic song that is playing in the club.

"Gentlemen prepare your necks for our main attraction, the seductive bat of Windwill Town. VAMPYRA." The man announces.

The song plays a little louder as everyone's attention turns to the stage. Tony and Andy remain in their seats, watching the stage as a spotlight flashes onto the entrance.

On the stage is a figure dressed entirely in black and hanging upside down from one of the swings. She slowly lowers her head, revealing her seductive face to the crowd. Her long, silky, jet black hair flows down from her face. Her midnight black eyes gaze eerily and seductively into the crowd as she gives the men a playful smile. Her beautiful and full cherry red lips glisten in the light as she licks her fangs provocatively to her audience.

Vampyra opens her arms, revealing what is hidden underneath the black cloak she is wearing. She shows the audience her perfectly toned abs and her thick and toned Columbian thighs and legs. She is wearing a pair of leather black booty shorts. Her firm and round breasts are held in a black leather bikini top with a silver lining of diamonds around the edges. She has very nice breasts; perfectly shaped and coming in a desirable and proportioned size. Her light brown Columbian skin is flawless, smooth and silky. This woman is truly the total package, radiating with a presence that is entirely her own.

Vampyra laughs lustfully, making the only sound in the whole room. Everyone's eyes and attention are completely glued on her, and she is feeding off of every minute of it. She grabs the bar and flips off of it, landing on the stage in a perfect split. She has taken off her cloak and left it hanging on the bar, revealing her outfit and black high heel boots.

Tony and Andy watch, like all the other men in the audience, completely hypnotized by Vampyra's beauty. Vampyra slowly glides across the stage on her hands and knees. She crawls over to one man in the crowd and she runs her hands against the side of his face. This man gazes at her in a trance as she lays on her back in front of him. She lifts herself up into a crab formation, catching his head with one hand and pressing her lips against his neck. She bites into his neck, giving him a hard and passionate hickey as everyone else in the audience stares into her opened legs. The man just sits there, completely lost in the moment. Vampyra lets him go, leaving behind a fresh hickey on his neck. He faints in his chair as she smiles and continues through the stage.

No one says a word as Vampyra stands up in the middle of the stage and starts grinding her hips and waist in front of the crowd. Tony and Andy watches her hips dreamily as they remain glued to their seats. Everyone in the room, even the other dancers, can't take their eyes off of Vampyra.

Vampyra grinds down to her hands and knees and then crawls into the crowd. The spotlight is still following her every move. She sits herself down on one man's lap and begins to crawl across the laps of every man in her path, rubbing their bodies and grinding herself against them during her journey.

Tony and Andy gaze longingly as Vampyra slides herself onto Andy's lap. Andy stares at her, completely hypnotized by her presence. She rubs herself against him and holds his head against her chest. He feels her hands slowly dipping into his pocket and into his wallet. She rubs his face against her chest and her lips against his neck. She pulls the money Tony had given him out of his wallet and smiles at Andy. She holds up Andy's head so that he is staring directly at her chest and face. He watches her place the fifty dollars between her breasts. Vampyra then tilts his head up so that he can look her in the eye.

"Thanks honey." Vampyra whispers with a smile.

Andy nods in response. Vampyra glides off of Andy and past Tony. Andy just sits there hypnotized, not even realizing that Vampyra has robbed him.

Vampyra walks across three other men to work her way back to the stage. She smiles and waves seductively to the crowd before pressing herself against one the bars. She grinds the bar while climbing up it. Vampyra reaches the top of the bar and wraps her legs around it. She hangs from the bar by her legs and exposes her fangs. Vampyra then folds her arms around herself to cover up.

Suddenly, the spot light in the strip club goes out and everything is once again dark.

Several moments later, all the lights turn on in the strip club and Vampyra, her cloak and any other trance of her is gone.

No one says a word as they stare at the stage as if Vampyra is still there. Tony and Andy stare at each other both men completely lost in the daze of Vampyra's smell and touch.

<C>   <E>   <O>

Shortly after Vampyra's dance ends, Tony and Andy leave the club and take the walk over to Andy's apartment building. Tony is still grinning at Andy, who still has the image of Vampyra in his mind.

"Dude she grinded you." Tony proudly exclaims, "You lucky son of a bitch."

Andy smiles, still smelling Vampyra's perfume and feeling the sensation of her flesh against his body. Andy savors this sensation as his grin widens. He has never felt anything that tantalizing before in his entire life, even when he had lost his virginity to Amy. His body aches with eager anticipation, begging him to go back to the club and find Vampyra.

Andy and Tony reach Andy's apartment building. They stop by the door and Andy takes out his keys to go inside. "If I were you I would never shower again." Tony says, still overly excited about Andy's achievement, "See, I told you would have fun tonight."

"Thanks Tony." Andy proudly declares with a smile, "I really needed this."

"You're welcome." Tony says, "I'll find out when she is working again and we'll go to the show. As long as I'm able to speak to her, I'm guaranteeing a lap dance for both of us."

"Do you want anything to drink or eat before you go?" Andy asks.

"No I'm cool." Tony replies, "I'll call you tomorrow after I speak to Amy. I'm sure she'll be pleased to go out with you on Friday."

"Thanks again for everything Tony." Andy says.

"You're welcome." Tony answers, shaking Andy's hands, "I'll call you later."

Tony heads back over to the train station in order to go home. Andy takes a deep breathe of fresh air, feeling more alive in this single moment than he has felt in a very long time. He feels strong, determined and energetic as he takes in the early morning air of Windwill Town, USA.

He enters the apartment building and takes his usual route to his apartment. Andy walks with his head held up high. He isn't worried about anything as he casually opens his door and enters his apartment.

He brushes his teeth, changes his clothes and goes to bed, placing his now empty wallet on the table next to him.

CHAPTER 4

Windwill Town University is the town's only college. A good majority of the students on this campus are actually in school to work hard and gain an education and an equal percentage of the professors are willing to help them. These people are the few living in Windwill Town who realize the value of education and see it as a way out of this secluded town and into the real, and possibly less dangerous, world around them.

However, citizens of Windwill Town still teach and attend this university, so there have been instances of rape, sexual harassment, crime and extensive drugs usage on campus. There are those students who have, whether willing or by force, performed "services" for their professors in order to get a good grade or to pass a class. Each dorm hall has at least one drug dealer living within its walls and there are plenty of wild parties that last all weekend long.

But doesn't this happen at all colleges?

Amy, just like Andy before he dropped out, attends Windwill Town University. She is a nursing major, hoping to one day become a doctor and finally leave this town. Amy lives in a pretty nice dorm on the campus with her roommate and best friend, Megan Lexie.

Megan, an attractive 22 year old woman with brown eyes and light brown hair and a nursing major as well, and Amy met when they became roommates in their freshman year.

Like Amy, Megan was born in Windwill Town and has lived here her whole life. Megan has a very dark past, having a mother who was hooker and a father who was a drunken crime lord, it became very easy for Megan to fall into a world of sex and heavy drug usage. In fact, Megan lost her virginity at 13 when she slept with one of her mother's clients, right after he had sex with her mother.

The feeling of an orgasm enthralled her at such a young age, and she yearned for that feeling everyday. She envied her mother and the amount of sex she was having and wanted to have just has much fun. Megan continued to have sex throughout her junior high and high school years with any man she could have regardless of his age, with no care or vision of a future beyond her actions. By living this lifestyle, it didn't take long for young Megan to discover drugs and alcohol. She found that she can have more sex if she is high or drunk, and in some cases, the orgasm will feel ten times better than if she is sober.

One day, because of her father's greed and carelessness, his own gang of thieves raided his home and murdered him and his wife right in front of 17 year old Megan's eyes. They then kidnapped Megan, beating and gang raping her for days until she was able to escape one week later. She was very lucky to have survived, and because of the physical, mental and emotional trauma her went through during that long week, Megan decided to turn her life around in a positive direction.

Amy and Megan walk through the campus heading for their dorm. Megan has always admired Amy's dedication to not give into the daily lures of Windwill Town. Megan always thought of Amy as a good influence on her, as well as one of the only true friends she has ever had. Megan values her friendship with Amy more than anything and will truly do anything for her.

"Has Pierre given you your phone back yet?" Megan asks, as the two walk through the grass near the dorm buildings.

"He won't give it back to me." Amy says, "He said if I really want it back, I will go into his pants and get it."

"He is stealing from you." Megan declares, "God, we have to find you a new job. Do you want me to try and get your phone back? I haven't done it in a while, but I'm still the greatest pick pocket this world has ever seen."

"I can take care of it." Amy sighs, "I'll talk to him when I go to work tomorrow."

"If you need me let me know." Megan assures, "I'll look out for you."

Amy and Megan arrive at the dorm building when they hear someone behind them calling out their names. They turn around and see Tony several feet away from them, running towards them. Amy and Megan stop so that Tony can catch up.

"Hey Tony." Megan greets, "What brings you here?"

"I have been chasing you guys and calling out your names for at least five minutes. You didn't hear me?" Tony asks.

"I'm sorry, we were talking." Amy says, "How have you been?"

"Excellent." Tony answers, flashing a smile, "And Andy has been doing okay as well." The sound of Andy's name brings immense happiness to Amy's heart.

"Is he with you?" Amy asks with an eager smile.

"No he should be at work by now." Tony says, looking at the time, "But listen, he wanted me to tell you that he really misses you and wants to spend time with you on Sunday."

Amy smiles like a school girl. "Oh, I'm off on Sunday." Amy exclaims excitedly.

Megan turns to Amy and laughs lightly. She then turns back to Tony. "I think that's a yes." Megan laughs.

"Excellent." Tony says, "I'll set it up and you two love birds will have the time of your lives in the fanciest restaurant that I can find."

"Good luck with the restaurant part." Megan replies with a laugh

"I'll talk to Andy tonight and call you tomorrow with the details." Tony says.

"You'll have to call my dorm." Amy says, "My boss took my phone and he refuses to give it back."

"Why did he do that?" Tony asks.

"Because he is a jack ass." Megan answers.

"What boss isn't?" Tony says, "Alright, I got to run. I'll talk to you ladies soon okay." Tony runs off to go to class. Megan turns to Amy, who is very excited about getting the opportunity to see Andy again.

"You see." Megan says, "Andy still loves of you and thinks about you. You should stop being so insecure all the time."

"I know." Amy says, "But, I really love him and it's hard when we never see each other." Megan places her arm around her friend and walks her into the dorm building

"That's what a vibrator is for." Megan laughs as the two women enter the building.

<C>   <E>   <O>

Andy suddenly finds himself standing in a small dimly lit room. He looks around the room in surprise, wondering why he is here. The only thing in the room with him is an old wooden chair which is standing in the middle of the room. Andy feels like calling for help, but his voice won't allow him to produce the words.

The door to the room opens and closes slowly. Andy's looks towards the doorway and notices that Vampyra has entered the room. Her hair is down and her lips are crimson red, full and moist. She is wearing a blood red lace corset with a matching thong and a pair of black laced tights. Andy stares hypnotically at her as she walks towards him. She lightly presses her hands against his chest and guides him to the chair in the middle of the room. His body is a puppet in Vampyra's hands, unable and unwilling to fight back against her will.

To Andy's surprise, Vampyra places him down on the chair. She turns around, pressing her hands onto his thighs and sliding herself to sit on his lap. Vampyra grinds her hips against his crotch. She presses her back against his chest and rubs the back of his head as she grabs his hands and places them on her waist.

Andy feels like he is in heaven as Vampyra slides his hands up her waist and presses his palms against her chest. She turns around to face him, his hands being guided around her waist. Vampyra licks his cheek as she twists her body around and holds him down in the chair.

He feels her breath against his face and the exotic smell of her perfume in his nostrils. He closes his eyes as Vampyra purses her lips and kisses him lightly.....

Andy's boss slams down hard against the table that Andy is leaning against in his sleep. Andy wakes up instantly, the vision of Vampyra gone and replaced with the unpleasant sight of Moore's Bar and Grill's kitchen.

Andy has, again, fallen asleep at work. He arrived at the warehouse three hours late this morning and was berated by his boss. Because he didn't get any sleep, he was barely able to function while carrying around heavy crates of metal. He had fallen asleep on the train, lucky to wake up with just in time to get out of the car before the doors closed on him. Now at the restaurant, he has fallen asleep in the kitchen area at least three times while working.

"What the hell is the matter with you?" the manager yells at Andy.

"I'm sorry sir, but I...." Andy begins to explain.

"Do I pay you to sleep or work?" the manager yells.

"Work." Andy says, "I'm…"

"So because you were sleeping, you don't deserve to get paid correct." The manager barks.

"Yes sir." Andy replies in defeat.

"Good, that's all I needed to know." The manager says, leaving the kitchen area to go to the office.

Andy watches him as the manager sits at his desk and logs onto the computer. He erases Andy's hours for the day from the time clock. Andy sighs in defeat and continues to work.

<C>   <E>   <O>

At around 2 am Andy's shift ends and he starts heading home. He fell asleep on the train again, and he once again dreamt about Vampyra. He can't understand why but all day and night, he hasn't been able to stop thinking about her.

Andy exits the train station and starts walking home, his body turning him to the direction where Fantasia's Surrender stands. Andy really wants to see Vampyra again. He doesn't fully understand why he wants to see her so much; Andy just knew that he has to see her. She is just so hypnotic. Andy's whole body pulls him towards the club, and as he gets closer, he is able to sense the smell of her perfume getting stronger.

By the time Andy arrives at Fantasia's Surrender, the doors are already closed. There is a sign on the door, informing any patrons that the club has reached their capacity on guest. Andy's stares blankly at the locked door, wondering if they have room for just one more inside.

Andy knocks on the door.

There is no answer.

Andy looks at the door in disappointment. Suddenly, Andy's exhaustion gets the better of him and he slumps against the wall in fatigue. His eyelids get very heavy and begin to close slowly as his body relaxes against the wall. He tries to stop himself from falling asleep, however he can't find the energy within him to do so.

A woman's scream suddenly startles Andy and he immediately becomes fully alert. Andy looks around, trying to figure out where the scream has come from. He hears the woman scream louder and then sounds of a struggle. Andy stands up straight and moves away from the club. It is

obvious to Andy that a woman is being attacked not
to far away from him.

"Down on your knees whore." A man says
as the woman's screams are suddenly muffled.
Andy can hear the laughter of several men as they
taunt their hostage.

His body begins to freeze with fear and he
stops, unable to think of what to do. The sounds are
coming from the far end of the side of the building,
only about twenty feet away from where Andy is
standing. Andy slowly walks toward the edge of
building, his mind telling him to run as his body
forces him forward.

He turns the corner and looks slowly toward
the site of the disturbance. There are four men
surrounding a woman. The woman is on her knees,
her arms held by two of the men. Another man has
a gun to the back of the woman's head while
another man is placing masking tape on her lips.
Andy can see the man holding the gun talking to the
woman, but he can't hear what he is saying.

Andy looks at the woman, wondering what
he should do. She doesn't seem afraid at all, but
she definitely doesn't enjoy what is happening to
her and she is helpless. Andy looks further over the
corner to get a better view of the woman's face.

Andy gasps lightly in shock. The woman is
Vampyra, Andy can recognize her from anywhere.
These thugs must have noticed her leaving the club
alone and decided to victimize her. Andy's body
starts shaking as the man who has placed the tape
on her lips pulls out a knife and slides it against her
chest.

"The boss says that you have been a bad
girl." The knife man says to her, "He told us to
make this very unpleasant for you." Vampyra says

something to the man, but it is muffled by the tape on her mouth.

Andy's body starts shaking again as he watches the men lay Vampyra flat on her chest. The gun man places the barrel of the gun against the back of her head as the knife man grabs her ankles. The two men holding her arms continue to hold her arms against her back.

Andy's mind starts racing, telling him to run away. There is also a small voice inside telling him to help her, or at least go into the strip club and inform a bouncer. He is so nervous that he starts to sweat, his mind completely unable to decide what to do. Andy's body decides to take action for itself, moving away form the side of the building so that he can get away....

"Leave her alone." Andy hears his voice say as he jumps out into the open.

The four men and Vampyra look at him in surprise and Andy realizes that he is no longer hidden by the shadows. The four men loosen their grip on Vampyra and stare at Andy with amusement in their eyes. The knife man rises and sizes Andy up. He lets out a load laugh when he decides that Andy isn't a threat to him. Andy remains still, nervous and astonished by his actions.

"You want to involve yourself in this buddy?" the gun man asks, "You want to play hero for this slut?"

"Yes." Andy stutters, "Or....ummm...I don't know."

"Kill him already so that we can..." The knife man says.

Vampyra interrupts him by kicking out her legs and slamming her boots into the man's knees. When the knife man falls to the ground, his knife is thrown out of his hands and lands on the sidewalk. The gun man turns to see what has happened only to have Vampyra kick his legs out from underneath him. He lands hard, his gun falling down the ground next to Vampyra.

The other two thugs try to strengthen their grip on Vampyra's arms, but she rolls away from their grasp. Vampyra reaches for the gun man's gun and fires at the two thugs' legs. They both fall down hard in pain as the knife man lounges forward. Vampyra kicks him in the face and he falls down as well.

Vampyra stands up and runs, grabbing a speechless Andy and bringing him with her. "Follow me." Vampyra suggests to him, but doesn't give Andy the option to refuse.

Andy follows Vampyra, and the two run through the streets together. He hears two of the men following them. Andy's heart races as he hears gun shots from behind him. "Don't look back just keep going." Vampyra says as she confidently runs into an alleyway.

Andy follows Vampyra as she runs into another alley and hides in a small dark corridor. Andy stumbles in there with her, the corridor so small that he can feel himself getting claustrophobic. Andy leans against the wall to catch his breath and Vampyra does the same.

"Don't make any sounds." Vampyra orders, looking outside of the alley to see if the thugs are nearby.

The knife man and gun man have lost them, running past the alley without even realizing Vampyra and Andy are hiding in there. Vampyra waits a few minutes and looks once again to see if everything is clear. The two men are gone.

Vampyra lets out a sigh of relief to relax herself and turns over to Andy. They are standing shoulder to shoulder in the alley. Andy's body is leaned against the wall. It took awhile, but he has been able to catch his breathe. However, his physical exhaustion is keeping him pressed against the wall and motionless.

To Vampyra, he looks like he is falling unconscious.

She taps him tightly, snapping him out of his trance. "Are you okay?" Vampyra asks, with some concern.

Andy nods to her and she leaves the alley and stretches out her body. Andy slumps out of the alley too and straightens himself up. Vampyra eyes him curiously as he stands before her physically and mentally fatigued.

"Don't I know you?" Vampyra asks, "Weren't you in the club last night?"

Andy nods in surprise, his body regaining some form of life. He can't believe that Vampyra recognized him and having her do so made his heart start pumping blood back into his system.

"You're the cheap gay guy." Vampyra laughs in realization, "The girls at the club were having a good laugh about you." Andy nods again, not paying any attention to what she has just said.

Vampyra gives him an inquiring stare, her mind racing with ideas. Andy stands there, not knowing what to say or do. "Thanks for saving me." Vampyra begins softly, "Those guys have been stalking me for a while and they aren't going to stop just because of this. They are probably going to go to my apartment and wait there for me."

Vampyra bites her lower lip and presses herself against Andy. Andy feels his whole body melting as he stares into her innocent and vulnerable eyes. His heart begins to beat faster, and his blood starts to get very warm.

"Do you live around here?" Vampyra whispers gently.

Andy's head nods "yes" very quickly and Vampyra smiles.

"Well I don't." Vampyra replies, "And I don't think it would be safe for me to go home with those mean men chasing me."

"You can stay with me for a while." Andy reluctantly offers before his brain can even register what he had just done. Vampyra giggles like a school girl and pats his chest, allowing her hands to glide down his arms. She takes his hand and Andy's body melts onto her delicate and precious palms.

"Okay my knight in shining armor." Vampyra giggles, "Take me to your castle."

Andy smiles and eagerly nods his head. They walk to Andy's apartment building together.

<C> <E> <O>

Along the outskirts of Windwill Town exists a world where the homes are actually very well maintained, the streets are litter and hooker free and the people actually have money. This is a very low crime zone, and consists not only of nice homes, but luxury style mansions as well. This area is the highly exclusive upper class world of Harold Square in Windwill Town.

Only the town's richest citizens (who are mostly crime lords, strip club owners as well as other legal and illegal business men) live in this world. For the most part, these people's homes are their offices, reducing the need to ever go into the poor part of Windwill Town. Because of the power the individual's living here have, very few people will ever dare enter this world and cause trouble. For the same reasons, not too many police officers will come over here and seek answers for a problem either.

One of the fortunate people who live in Harold Square is a man by the name of Roman Castle. Currently, Roman Castle is sitting in his luxury style living room, smoking a cigar while staring into the eyes of a man who is sitting across from him. The bright light of the rising sun shines inside of his living room. Roman is staring off into the sky, extremely calm, collected and casual in demeanor. The other man in the room with Roman is sitting nervously in his chair, watching Roman twirl a pistol in his hands while smiling and smoking.

Roman Castle is a very muscular and tall black man of 45 years of age. His black eyes pierce into the other man's soul, even though he isn't looking at him directly, and his lips show off a twisted grin even with the cigar in his mouth. Roman's large hand embraces the pistol, toying with it as if it is a catnip mouse. The other man, a skinny white man with glasses, is sweating profusely as Roman takes another drag off of his cigar.

"So you are telling me that I can't own your casino." Roman repeats, "Even though I have the funds to buy it."

"This casino has been in my family for years.' The man pleads, "You can't just buy it from me."

"All I want to do is share in the money that your establishment makes." Roman says politely, "Are you a greedy man Mr. Polanski?"

"No no, not at all Mr. Castle but I..." Mr. Polanski explains.

"Then you shouldn't have any problem accepting my generous offer of $20,000 for the ownership of your business." Roman interrupts, still twirling the gun and now looking directly at Mr. Polanski.

"I run a billion dollar business Mr. Castle. You can't possibly buy it for only $20,000 dollars, it isn't right or fair." Mr. Polanski states.

"Are you insulting my generosity Mr. Polanski?" Roman asks, still maintaining his friendly and calm persona.

"No it is just that..." Mr. Polanski explains.

"Perhaps generosity is the wrong way to do business." Roman states. In one fluid motion, Roman grips the gun and fires a bullet into Mr. Polanski's forehead. Mr. Polanski dies instantly, the chair falling to the floor along with Polanski's headless body.

"Perhaps, a hostile take over is the only alternative." Roman says, lighting another cigar and standing up from his chair.

Roman Castle is the most dangerous criminal in Windwill Town. He pretty much owns every drug ring, prostitution ring, gambling ring and crime ring in the town and it has been this way for a number of years.

Having grown up on the streets of Windwill Town, Roman Castle learned at an early age how to take care of himself in this harsh world. As he grew older, he networked with all the right people, learning the crime business and the inner workings of the town's illegal and legal businesses. When he turned 25 years old, Roman used all of his knowledge and experience to kill those who created him. He took over their businesses and used the contacts he had gained from them, as well as new ones, to keep himself one of the richest and most feared men in Windwill Town's history.

Roman Castle is completely untouchable by the law and anyone else for that matter. Not bad for a scrawny orphan from the streets.

Roman takes some towels and leisurely throws them on top of Mr. Polanski's dead body. As Roman covers the fresh corpse, a man in a trench coat and dark glasses enters the living room. This man is the knife man who attacked Vampyra at the strip club.

"Mr. Castle I…." the man says.

"Great Drew, you are here." Roman greets, placing the last towel on top of Mr. Polanski's blown apart head, "Clean this up for me will you. I don't want the blood to stain my carpet."

"I'll get right on it sir." Drew says, "But I have to tell you about Tessa."

The sound of Tessa's name runs a cold chill of anger up Roman's spine. He turns toward Drew as memories of Tessa flood his mind. "How is Tessa doing these days?" Roman asks angrily, rubbing his hands together. As he does this, his nine finger rings rub together as well.

"She got away sir." Drew informs, "Some man helped her escape."

"Tessa has a new man in her life." Roman replies staring at himself in the mirror.

"Yes sir." Drew continues, "I don't know who this man is but…"

"Find out everything there is to know about Tessa's new boyfriend." Roman orders, "And when you do, bring them both to me. I want back what rightfully belongs to me."

"Yes sir." Drew says, leaving the living room without another word. The door closes behind him and Roman simply takes another drag out of his cigar.

CHAPTER 5

Andy stirs in his bed, slowly rising as he feels the light of the sky shine on his face. Andy rubs his eyes and slowly looks at the time on his alarm clock.

10 am.

Andy shoots up quickly. He was supposed to be at work an hour ago. Instinctively, he rises from his bed and heads to the bathroom door, which for some reason is closed.

His telephone rings, stopping him in his tracks. Andy knew it has to be his boss at the warehouse calling him. Andy watches the phone like a deer in headlights, the ringing getting louder and longer in his head. He wonders whether he should answer it or not, fearing what would happen if he went with either option.

Vampyra steps out of Andy's bathroom very casually, wrapped in a towel and drying her hair. With no hesitation in motion, she casually strolls over to Andy's home phone. She leisurely picks up the phone to answer the call as if it is her phone she is answering. Andy watches her in complete shock.

"Hello." Vampyra says.

Andy's boss pauses, surprised to hear a woman's voice answer the phone. "Who is this?" Andy's warehouse boss screams into the phone, "Where is Andy? He is late."

"I'm Andy's sister." Vampyra replies sadly, "I'm sorry but we tried to call earlier. There has been a family emergency this morning. Our mother is very sick and we have to go to the hospital."

"I don't care about Andy's mother." The boss yells, "I need a warehouse worker. Tell that boy to get his ass..."

"Excuse me sir, this is my family you're talking out." Vampyra whines, "How could you be so cruel?"

Vampyra pretends to cry, and before the boss can reply back, she hangs up the phone in his face. As soon as the connection is broken, Vampyra charade ends and she turns to Andy. She flashes him a friendly smile and she goes back to drying her hair.

Andy is still standing by his bathroom door, a few feet away from Vampyra. He is completely dumbfounded, his brain not fully registered what has happened yet. For some reason none only to Vampyra, he isn't going to work today.

"Why....why did you do that?" Andy asks hesitantly.

Vampyra laughs. "You can't go to work." She replies, "You and I have to talk."

"About what?" Andy asks, very confused.

Vampyra walks up to Andy and presses herself against him. Andy can feel the wet towel against his chest as Vampyra holds his waist. His body is completely frozen with bewilderment as he stares into Vampyra's black eyes.

"I need help." Vampyra whispers, "And you seem to be the only person who wants to help me. You do want to help me right?"

Andy's brain is still having trouble registering what is going on. Everything is happening so fast for him to understand. However, feeling the warmth transferring between he and Vampyra's bodies is distracting him form any kind of logical thinking. "I don't know if I can..." Andy replies hesitantly.

Vampyra smiles and lightly taps Andy's face. "Don't just stand there." Vampyra laughs playfully, "Go take a shower and get dressed, we have fun day ahead of us."

Without another word, Vampyra lets go off Andy. She casually goes back to drying her hair, turning her back towards Andy. Andy is still standing in his position, wondering why he is not going to work today and what Vampyra is thinking about.

Andy walks slowly into his bathroom and closes the door. He starts the water in the shower and removes his clothes. He steps into the shower and starts to bath.

When Vampyra hears the running water in the shower, she immediately stops drying her hair. She walks to Andy's night table and grabs his wallet. Vampyra checks Andy's wallet and is disappointed when she discovers that it is empty. She sighs and places the wallet down and walks over to grab a bra from her bag.

After about an hour, Andy and Vampyra are ready to leave. Andy's phone rings as soon as they walk out of the door. The answer machine picks up the call after several rings. The phone call is from Tony, who leaves his message on the machine.

"Hey buddy it's Tony. Listen, I talked to Amy and she is available on Friday. I took the liberty of setting up reservations for you and Amy to go out to dinner. Call me later man."

<C>   <E>   <O>

"By the way, you can call me Tessa, that's my real name." Vampyra says.

"Okay Vamp…Tessa." Andy stumbles, as Vampyra smiles.

After leaving Andy's apartment, Tessa takes Andy over to Stalloni's Breakfast Stop, a friendly 24 hour diner in the neighborhood. It is still early in the afternoon, so the neighborhood is pretty quiet and inactive. Stalloni's is occupied with a few customers who are all having a cheap but fulfilling brunch in the diner. The owner of the diner, Harvey Stalloni tries to accommodate for the fact that most people in the neighborhood are poor, so he makes his prices as fair as possible for everyone without sacrificing quality and profit.

Tessa and Andy walk into the diner and sit down at a booth. They take the menus and read them over for a moment. The waiter comes and greets them after a few minutes, and asks them if they are ready to order. Tessa orders a fruit and vegetable salad with a glass of pineapple juice and Andy orders pancakes with syrup and a glass of apple juice. Andy is particularly quiet and nervous, while waiting for the food to come, unable to think of anything to say to Tessa. When they receive their food and start eating, Andy finally decides to utter a sentence.

"Who is chasing you?" Andy asks.

"A man by the name of Roman Castle." Tessa explains, "My father worked for him as a business manager. After years of loyal service to the company, my father lost a business deal which cost Roman thousands of dollars. Roman wanted his money back, but my father couldn't afford to pay. After a week, Roman had his thugs rob my father's home, stealing all of his money and belongings and then kidnapping me as an additional form of payment. Roman sold what he stole from my family and then decided to raise the rest of the money by selling me as a prostitute. My father tried to rescue me, but he and my mother were caught and murdered."

"That's terrible." Andy exclaims, a wave of sympathy washing over him, "How did you get away?'

"I have been sneaking out to work at the strip club for a few months in order to raise the money to run away." Tessa explains, "Since Roman killed my parents, I have no family in this town to help me. A few weeks ago, I finally had enough money to be free and that night, I ran away for good. When Roman realized I was gone, he sent his thugs to find me and I have been avoiding them ever since."

Tessa takes a small box out of her pocket. "The last time I saw my dad, he gave me this." Tessa says, giving the box to Andy. Andy takes the box and tries to open it, but Tessa stops him. "Please don't open it." Tessa begs, "It is very delicate." Andy honors Tessa's wish.

"In that box is an heirloom that has been passed down through my family for generations." Tessa continues, "My father gave it to me so that I'll have the strength to continue living while under Roman's control. He said that as long as I have this, my parents and God will always protect me. The heirloom is worth allot of money and Roman wants to sell it and make more money off of me and my family."

Andy stares into Tessa's innocent eyes, feeling incredible sympathy for the situation that Tessa has been forced into. He has never heard such a tragic story in his life, and he can feel a tear ready to fall from his eyes. He admires the genuine sincerity in her voice as she takes his hand and holds it tightly for comfort and strength.

"He made me do allot of things for him that I don't want to ever do again." Tessa says, "And if he sells this heirloom, I'll lose the last thing that connects me to my parents."

"Why can't you go to the police?" Andy asks.

"You know the police around here, they are all crooked cops." Tessa informs, "In a week or two, I'll have enough money to move to Seattle and find my grandparents. Roman will never find me there and I'll have an opportunity at a new life. I need someone to protect me from Roman until I can move."

Andy's mind absorbs all the information he has been given. He feels bad for Tessa, and deep inside, he truly wants to help her. Andy has always wanted to make a difference in someone's life, and this seems like an opportunity for him to do so.

But can Andy really be a bodyguard?

"I'll do what I can, but I have to work and…" Andy hesitantly says.

"You don't have to go to your job remember." Tessa insists, "Your mother is sick in the hospital and needs your care." Andy nods slowly, as Tessa smiles. Andy just happens to look at the time. It is 2 pm and he has to be at Moore's Bar and Grill at 4 pm.

"I have two jobs and if I don't leave now I'm going to be late to my second one." Andy says.

"You can't go to work." Tessa insists, "You have to go to the club with me and protect me. They know where I work and they're going to be back."

Can Andy really be a bodyguard? The only fights he has ever been in involved him having his ass kicked and robbed in various places across the town. He can barely defend himself in a confrontation; another person would be too much to deal with.

"I don't know if I should." Andy says, "I can't lose my job and if I don't go in today...."

"I'll pay you." Tessa pleads desperately, grasping his hands, "Anything I make tonight is yours, just please be there for me."

Andy stares into her eyes, seeing her helplessness and desperation rising. He has the opportunity to help some one who genuinely needs it. The good man within Andy is telling him that can't abandon Tessa, or anyone else, in a time of need.

"Okay I'll go with you tonight." Andy decides, "But I don't know how much of a help I'll be."

"Just watch over me while I'm on stage." Tessa replies very relieved, "And don't let them hurt me."

"Alright." Andy says, trying to sound confident, "I'll do what I can."

"Oh God, thank you." Tessa says, hugging Andy. Andy holds her, feeling a sense of security within her. Having her believe in him made him feel a little more confident about helping her out. Tessa lets him go, and he can tell by looking into her eyes that his presence around her has taken a huge burden off her shoulders.

"We have to go back to my place and get my stuff." Tessa says, "I work tonight and I'm going to need some clothes for the week."

"Okay." Andy answers with a bit more confidence then before.

Tessa calls for the check and moments later, the waiter arrives with it. Tessa pulls money (the

50 she had stolen from Andy at the club tow nights ago) out of her bra and pays the bill.

<C>   <E>   <O>

After leaving the diner, Tessa and Andy take the train to Tessa's apartment. The apartment, which is a very upper class loft, has been ransacked. Someone, possibly the four thugs who attacked her last night, went into the apartment to look for something. Andy helps Tessa pack some of her clothes into one suitcase so that she will have something to wear while staying at Andy's apartment.

They carry the suitcase, or rather Andy carries the suitcase, back over to Andy's apartment. When they arrive at his apartment, Andy drops Tessa's suitcase in front of the door and quickly fiddles through his keys. Tessa waits for him to open the door wondering why Andy is rushing to go inside. When Andy finds the right key, Mr. McGuckin's door opens and the greasy man wobbles out of his apartment.

"I've been looking for you all day Hair Comb." McGuckin growls, stomping towards Andy, "Where is my….."

Mr. McGuckin sees Tessa and freezes in his tracks. Tessa and Andy look at him, Andy in fear and Tessa in disgust. McGuckin grins and licks his lips at the sight of Tessa.

"I'm sorry about the rent but…" Andy pleads.

"Who's your friend?" McGuckin asks, droll coming out of his mouth and soiling his beard as he stares lustfully at Tessa. Tessa smiles at him and walks closer to him.

"I'm his girlfriend." Tessa grins, "Or maybe I should say fuck buddy."

Tessa moves within arms distance of Mr. McGuckin, who is still drooling and is now rubbing his privates. Tessa's face shows visible disgust that the bearded Irish man doesn't seem to realize. Andy just looks on in surprise and curiosity at Tessa's words.

"I didn't know you had a fuck buddy Hair Comb." McGuckin chuckles at Andy, while drooling over Tessa.

"I didn't either." Andy answers in surprise. Tessa looks at Andy and then back at McGuckin.

"How much rent does Andy owe you sexy?" Tessa asks. McGuckin smiles at Tessa, obviously turned on by her.

"Two hundred and fifty dollars candy ass." McGuckin grins, trying to impress Tessa with the charm of a container of lard.

Tessa smiles. "Well, that seems like a lot to give you all at once." Tessa explains, "Especially since Andy doesn't have allot of time to work because he's been having so much sex with me."

"I can have a lot of sex with you." McGuckin drools with a horny grin, "I have a bigger cock than Hair Comb a big load of semen for you to swallow."

"Tempting offer." Tessa replies in disgust, "How about this baby? You stop charging Andy rent, and I'll come by your apartment and give you everything I give Andy. Maybe a little more, if you're a good boy."

Tessa leans in forward for a kiss, much to Mr. McGuckin's liking. Andy's eyes open wide in surprise and disgust. Tessa's lips are only inches away from McGuckin's as he moves closer to kiss her. Tessa stops him and smiles.

"Not yet." Tessa purrs, "I want you ready for me."

"Oh my cock is hard." McGuckin moans, still rubbing his privates in front of Tessa. He quickly heads into his apartment, "Keep that pussy wet for me."

"I'll wear something sexy just for you tiger." Tessa coos as McGuckin closes his door while dropping his pants. When McGuckin's door shuts, Tessa's smile fades to a look of complete repulsion. Andy stares at Tessa and she turns towards him with a sigh.

"Are you actually going to…" Andy slowly asks.

"Hell no." Tessa snaps, "I'm taking a shower."

Tessa walks into Andy's apartment. Tessa enters the bathroom and closes the door behind her. Andy carries Tessa's suitcase into his apartment and closes the front door. He places the suitcase in the corner by the bathroom and sits down on his couch. His body starts to relax against the couch. Carrying Tessa's luggage is nothing like a crate full of metal objects, but his weakened body still felt exhaustion from the trip. Andy closes his eyes slowly, the only sound in his apartment coming from the running water in his bathroom.....

The sound of Andy's phone ringing snaps him out of his trance. Andy turns over to the phone and picks up the receiver.

"Hello." Andy answers.

"Andy, finally I got a hold of you." Tony says on the other end, "Did you get my message?"

Andy checks his messages and notices that there are 2 messages on his machine.

"I didn't get the messages." Andy lies, "I just got home from work and I'm getting ready to go to the restaurant."

"Well listen I talked to Amy and I set up reservations for the two of you to have dinner at Oceanside River tomorrow at 8 pm." Tony says, "Do you still have the fifty dollars I gave you at the strip club?"

Andy checks his wallet and realizes that it is empty. He thinks for a moment, trying to remember if he had spent it already. Knowing Andy, it is more likely that he lost it somewhere.

"Yes." Andy lies to Tony again

"Good." Tony says, "Use that to pay for the diner. As you know, Amy is a big fan of seafood, so she will love the surprise."

"Okay I will." Andy says, hearing the shower water turning off in the bathroom, "I have to go I..."

"Andy are you ready yet?" Tessa calls from the bathroom. Andy jumps, dropping the phone and hoping that Tony didn't hear Tessa's voice. Andy frantically picks up the phone. "Andy are you ready yet?" Tessa asks again as Andy coughs into the receiver to hide her voice.

"Are you okay Andy?" Tony asks with concern, hearing the coughing and phone dropping in the background.

"Yeah I just dropped the phone that's all, and I'm pretty sick." Andy replies, coughing again.

"Andy I have to go to work." Tessa whines, "Come on answer me Andy. You are still there right? You didn't leave me did you?"

"Who is that Andy?" Tony laughs, jokingly, "I hear someone. Do you have a special friend over?"

"No." Andy says, quickly, "Look Tony, I have to go to work I'm going to be late."

"Alright." Tony laughs, "Just remember, Oceanside River at 8 pm tomorrow."

"I will." Andy says, "Goodbye." Andy hangs up the phone and lets out a sigh of relief. Tessa walks out of the bathroom fully clothed and with her hands on her hips.

"Andy why didn't you answer me?" Tessa asks, looking afraid and annoyed at the same time, "I thought something had happened to you."

Andy has never been good at confrontations, so having Tessa approach him like this is very uncomfortable for him. "I... uh.... I'm sorry." Andy stutters.

"You can't scare me like that Andy, I have killers after me." Tessa pouts. Andy's voice finally returns to him.

"I'm sorry I really am, I was just on the phone." Andy says.

"Please don't do that again." Tessa says. Tessa walks to the door and grabs her bag and coat, "We have to leave now. I have a show that starts at 8pm and I can't be late."

"Okay." Andy answers. He collects himself, thankful that the confrontation is over. Andy grabs his coat and puts it on and Tessa does the same. He and Tessa head out of his apartment and over to the strip club.

<C>   <E>   <O>

Never in Andy's life has he felt so displaced and uncomfortable around a group of people.

Andy nervously looks around the club, feeling really awkward as he watches giddy men of all ages gawking over the women and the women completely ignoring him. Tessa had told the women to leave Andy alone because he is there on a mission to protect her and can't be distracted. Since they all remembered Andy from the other night, the strippers are all more than happy to obey Tessa's wishes. Also, since Andy's is not a woman, there isn't a guy in the club who will even think about approaching him, much less strike up a conversation with him.

Look at these men, they are being manipulated and taken advantage of by gorgeous women that they will never touch without giving up all of their cash. As for the women, how degrading must it be for a woman to sell herself, for any amount of money, to a man who doesn't think of her as anything more than sexual pleasure. Where is the dignity and self respect in offering yourself to random men in exchange for anything?

As Andy watches the crowd, he slowly begins to realize one thing; the human race is a materialistic, superficial and emotionless breed.

But who can blame them. As easy as it is in this town to have sex, is it really a man's fault that he has absolutely no respect for women. There are more employed prostitutes and strippers in Windwill Town than employed wives and single mothers. In addition to that, there are so many women in town who are just plain sluts; willing to spread their legs and have sex with any man or woman who comes along, whether they are being paid or not.

Andy really wishes that Vampyra will hit the stage soon so that he can go home.

Andy has been sitting in front of the stage for two hours while Vampyra readies herself in the dressing room doing whatever a dancer does before she hits the stage. Adding to Andy's feelings of uneasiness in the strip club is the absolute fact that he has no idea how he will protect Vampyra if a situation does occur.

Shouldn't he be in the back to protect her? What if these guys invaded the dressing rooms and hurt her? Maybe he should try to get backstage just to check on her? Or maybe he should sit here and wait for them to come in through the front door? Maybe they'll come in through the back door. Should he be waiting by the back door in case they come in through the back door...

Questions are racing through Andy's mind, and unfortunately, the answers aren't coming out quick enough.

The lights go out, and the announcer introduces Vampyra to the stage. Andy watches Vampyra dance on stage, the world around him becoming a blur as she moves and twists her body. She has again, and as always, captivated the audience with her stunning presence. Everyone in the club is hypnotized by Vampyra's body, beauty and sexual energy and she is taking in all of her power like the mythical succubus feasting on her prey.

There is someone in the crowd immune to Vampyra's passion. A man sits in the crowd of hypnotized men with a camera, taking pictures of Vampyra and Andy. When Vampyra finishes her act and the lights turn back on, the man smiles and leaves the strip club.

CHAPTER 6

Having taken enough pictures to satisfy his needs, Drew returns to Roman's mansion to print them out. Roman sent Drew to spy on Tessa and to also figure out who Andy is and how much of a threat he is. Roman wants a full report in the morning, so Drew spent the rest of the night preparing himself for this important meeting.

It is now the next morning, and Roman has called Drew into his office for their meeting. Drew enters Roman's study, finding him already sitting in the room and smoking a fresh cigar. Drew takes a seat in the chair in front of Roman's desk and sits down.

"I got the pictures boss." Drew informs as he hands the photos he'd taken at the strip club over to Roman. Roman eyes the pictures, staring holes through them as he glares at Andy and Tessa. He takes a drag out of his cigar before speaking.

"Are you sure this is her boy toy?" Roman asks, curiously looking at the photos, "He doesn't look like Tessa's type."

"She walked into the club with him." Drew explains, pointing out the evidence in the photos, "He kept a very watchful eye on her and the entire club. I'm surprised that he didn't notice me."

"What is his name?" Roman asks, still looking at the pictures, "What does he do? Who is he that makes him so important to my little Tessa?"

"I'll start asking around Mr. Castle." Drew offers, "Someone has to know him."

Roman stares at a face shot of Tessa. Tessa has a stray strand of hair in her mouth and she is biting lightly on it. Her dark eyes glisten as just seductively in the photo as it does in real life. Roman licks his lips as he looks at the picture.

"I want to see her." Roman tells Drew, "She has been away from me for too long." Roman can't take his eyes off of her photo, too mesmerized by her beauty to look away.

"She is working tonight boss." Drew says, "Your schedule is clear."

Roman continues to stare at the photo in silence, not really paying attention to what Drew has just said. Roman takes his cigar and places it right between Tessa's eyes in the photo. He watches the picture burn slowly in his hands, finding enjoyment out of Tessa's sexy face melt in his hand.

"Take me to her." Roman orders Drew.

<C>   <E>   <O>

Amy looks at herself in the mirror, carefully analyzing her outfit as Megan watches her from her bed. Megan isn't a girlie girl at all. She isn't the type of girl who would stand in front of a mirror for hours before a date. She wouldn't sit in the bathroom for hours doing her hair and make up before going on a date either. Megan will just brush her hair, throw on a t-shirt and jeans, and leave the house.

Nice, simple, can't possibly go wrong

So having to watch Amy try on four different outfits in the past hour and half and not like anyone of them even though they all looked fine on her is boarding on the line of inhumane torture for Megan.

"You do realize that whatever you wear, Andy is going to love the way it looks on you?"

Megan tells her friend as she watches Amy model
the fifth outfit in the mirror.

Amy looks at her nervously from the mirror.
"I have to look really good." Amy reasons, "I
haven't seen Andy in such a long time and he will
want me….."

"Bare naked and laying on your back."
Megan remarks with a smirk

Amy looks at Megan and laughs a little bit.
Megan smiles and leaves her bed. She stands
behind her friend, pointing Amy towards the mirror
and gently holding her shoulders.

"You look fine." Megan reassures Amy,
"Andy doesn't care about what clothes you wear.
He will love you no matter what, so there is no need
to create all this trouble."

Megan pauses so that Amy can absorb
everything that she has said. Amy looks at herself
in the mirror, still feeling slightly unsure about what
she is wearing. Megan notices this uncertainty and
smiles at her friend.

"If you try on another outfit." Megan begins
softly, "I'm going to kill you."

Amy looks at herself one more time.
"Okay." Amy says, "I'm ready I can go."

"Thank God." Megan sighs with relief,
letting go of Amy and walking over to her bed. She
lays out on her bed and opens a magazine. "I didn't
know what I would have done if threatening your
life didn't work." Megan says, "Do you want me to
go with you?"

"I can handle it." Amy replies, "I'm so
excited about tonight. I can't wait to see him."

"You won't see him if you don't leave
now." Megan says, "You're going to be late. You
are supposed to meet him at 8 pm."

Amy takes one more look in the mirror and smiles in satisfaction. She reaches for her jacket and heads for the door. Amy opens the door and turns over to Megan. "Thank you for everything Megan." Amy says, "What would I do without you?"

"You would be trying on more outfits." Megan laughs with a smile, "Good bye."

Amy blows a kiss to her friend and walks out of the room.

<C> <E> <O>

Just like the night before, Andy finds himself once again in the front row at Fantasia's Surrender. He felt slightly less uncomfortable now then before, but only because of the safety in his solitude. He felt pretty good about the fact that nobody will approach him for anything. However, this still didn't keep him from wanting to leave as soon as possible.

At the moment, Tessa is on stage performing her last routine. After twenty minutes, Tessa leaves the stage, much to the dismay of her tantalized male audience. She disappears backstage where she will change into another outfit.

When the lights come back on, Andy looks up at the time. It is 11 pm, and Vampyra had told Andy that she would be walking the floor tonight for an extra hour, flirting with the men and giving out lap dances at her own discretion. Vampyra never does lap dances, but she had told Andy that she will try to make a little extra money to give to Andy for staying in the club with her.

Vampyra hasn't paid Andy yet and she feels pretty bad about it.

"Excuse me sir, but you have to come with me." a man says to Andy.

Andy turns around in surprise, noticing that there is a man standing behind him. Andy looks up at this man and notices that another man is standing with him. Each man is wearing a police uniform with a hat and dark glasses. The hat and sunglasses are hiding their faces very well. The man who had spoken to Andy is holding up a badge to identify himself as a police officer.

"Did I do something wrong officers?" Andy asks, as the officers stare down at him with a cold gaze.

"We need to ask you some questions sir." The officer holding the badge says, "Would you please step outside with us?"

"Okay." Andy cooperatively replies.

He stands up from his chair and walks outside with the officers. He keeps looking back into the crowd, watching for Vampyra to come out. Should he really be leaving Vampyra's side when there are killers after her?

The officers take Andy outside and into the parking lot of the strip club. Andy turns towards the strip club, wondering if Vampyra is going to be okay. If she gets hurt, Andy will have failed his job.

Andy will have failed her.

One of the officers takes out his night stick and hits Andy in the back of the head so swiftly that Andy doesn't even realize what has hit him. Andy's eyes fade to black and he falls down to the sidewalk.

<C>   <E>   <O>

Where the hell is he?

Vampyra leaves the back room and looks toward where Andy is supposed to be sitting. She places her hands on her hips in disgust as she glares at the empty seat. She had specifically told him to sit there and not move and now the chair is empty. None of the other dancers would have possibly given a broke dumb ass like Andy a lap dance, so where the hell is he?

Vampyra walks into the crowd, trying to see if maybe the idiot just got lost in the club. Some men approach her with money and ask for a lap dance and she waves them away. Vampyra NEVER does lap dances. She is VAMPYRA and VAMPYRA is not going to dance on any men's lap for any amount of money, especially a miserable middle aged pervert waving dollars around in a strip club.

Vampyra stops suddenly when she feels a pair of large hands grasp her hips and pull her backwards. She finds her back pressed up against a tall man's muscular body. She would have kneed the man in the crotch if she not had instantly recognized his touch.

Tessa moans softly, pressing the back of her head against Roman Castle's chest. Roman runs his hand up Tessa's chest and grasps her neck firmly. He tilts her head up and plants his lips on hers, kissing her passionately as Tessa presses herself against him. It is a kiss that Tessa knows very well, and quite honestly, truly missed.

No one can ever please her the way Roman Castle can.

Roman violently pulls Tessa off of him and turns her towards him so that they are face to face. "Give me a lap dance whore." Roman snarls, roughly holding Vampyra's waist. She smirks mockingly at him.

"You haven't seen me in months and that's all you can say to me?" Vampyra asks.

"Now!" Roman demands, as he firmly grasps Vampyra's wrists and pulls her towards his body.

"Give me fifty dollars." Vampyra snaps back at Roman while trying to fight out of his grasp.

He smiles evilly at her, admiring her spunk.

"NOW!!!!!!" Roman growls.

He forces her into one of the lap dance rooms, closing and locking the door behind them. None of the bouncers pay them any mind, all of them knowing very well that they do not take on Roman Castle for any reason.

Roman swings Vampyra over to the chair like a rag doll and stands in front of it. Vampyra collects herself and glares at him angrily, grabbing him by the collar of his shirt as hard as she can. Roman allows her to control him as she guides him over to the chair.

"You want a lap dance." Vampyra smiles angrily, "I'll give you one."

Vampyra slams Roman down on the seat and sits down on his lap, running her hands along his chest while grinding her hips against his. Roman sits like a gentlemen, his hands on the legs of the chair as he watches Vampyra work him.

Despite her anger, she keeps her body movements slow, intimate and rhythmic. She can feel her body relaxing and her anger settling, and she knows for a fact that Roman's has subsided for the moment as well. She always finds comfort in Roman's presence, so she allows her body to relax so she can please him the way he desires.

No woman can every please Roman the way Tessa can.

"So what are you doing here anyway?" Vampyra asks, "Scouting for talent."

"The better question would be why you are here." Roman replies, "You are too hot of a product for this place."

Vampyra presses her chest against Roman's chest and holds him tightly against her body. "I'm too hot for anyone to handle." Vampyra whispers with the grin, "Even a man as big as you are."

Roman's tongue attempts to graze against Vampyra's chest. She pulls herself away from him quickly while grinning playfully at him. "No touching Roman." Vampyra says softly, "You don't want to get kicked out."

"Is that a threat?" Roman asks casually.

Vampyra presses her back against Roman's chest and grinds her ass against his crotch. She slowly grasps the back of his head, tilting it down so that he can see inside her corset.

"That depends honey." Vampyra whispers, "Why are you really here?"

"My men tell me that you have a new man in your life." Roman says as Vampyra slides herself between Roman's legs. She opens them and stares into his eyes, running her hands along his inner thighs. Roman smiles at her to show that he is enjoying her touch.

"And he's more of man then you'll ever be." Vampyra grins as she runs her hand between his legs.

"Do tell." Roman says.

He licks his lips and glares at her on her knees between his legs. He definitely never gets tired of seeing his little Tessa on her knees, and he definitely misses having his little Tessa holding his crotch. Seeing her like this is causing him to relive all those moments of pleasure all over again.

"He's is an amateur boxer." Vampyra explains, "A black belt in karate and master of jujitsu." Vampyra firmly grips the bulge in Roman's pants and brings her face closer to his zipper. "And his dick is much bigger than yours." Vampyra smirks with a seductive bite on her lip.

"Now that's hitting below the belt." Roman casually replies as his hand moves towards the back of Vampyra's head, "You can make it up to me."

Vampyra lets him go and stands up. She places her right leg on his shoulder and bends her knees to pull her crotch close to Roman's face. Roman holds her waist as she places her hands on his head.

"Sorry Roman, I have a real man now." Vampyra teases, "I'm not yours anymore."

"Your man has a very impressive resume." Roman tells her, his face just inches away from Vampyra's inner thighs, "But he doesn't at all look like he can satisfy you."

"He's doing a fine job." Vampyra says, slithering her legs off of Roman's shoulder and slowly placing herself on his lap, "Really Roman, you should get over me. You are never going to get me back, or anything else that I have that's yours."

Suddenly, Roman violently grabs his little Tessa and pins her against the wall. Tessa knows Roman to be this way, calm and collected one second, violent and angry the other. Even after all these years, it still scares her to have Roman forcefully place his hands on her, and his massive size advantage does not help matters either.

Roman holds her wrists behind her with one hand as his other hand grasps Tessa's face. Tessa tries to fight back against him, but as usual, her efforts are futile. He is definitely hurting her, holding her as if she is of comparable size and strength. He places his thumb on her lips and he laughs in her terrified face.

"I will always have you Tessa." Roman mocks, "As conniving and strong as you are, you will never be rid of me. You need me you ungrateful bitch, and you know that no matter how far you run, I will always find you."

Roman presses his hands forcefully against her chest. His strength is so powerful, Tessa can feel her breathing pattern slowing down, as if her lungs are caving in underneath Roman's powerful grasp. "You have something of mine that isn't yours and I want it back." Roman snarls at Tessa.

"I just wanted to…." Tessa chokes out and cries at Roman

"I CAN KILL RIGHT NOW YOU FILTHY SLUT!!!!" Roman yells into Tessa's face, "Submit yourself to me."

"Go to hell." Tessa chokes back at Roman. Roman smiles and punches Tessa in the face. He lets her go and Tessa falls to the floor, holding her bruise as Roman towers over her in triumph. The last time Roman hit Tessa, the strength of the blow was enough to knock her unconscious. He definitely held back his brawn this time.

"Without me Tessa you are nothing but a desperate mouse looking for a meal." Roman growls as he stands over her with his fists clenched. Tessa can hear the sounds of his nine finger rings clanging together as his knuckles begin to get white.

"Let's see you dance on stage with two broken legs." Roman growls at her.

Roman moves to grab Tessa but she crawls away and cowers into a corner. "Don't touch me." Tessa cries, clutching herself and backing into the corner, "Don't ever touch me again." Roman smiles as he pulls himself back from his little Tessa.

"As strong as you are, you were never able to defeat me." Roman taunts, "I'll give you the win this time. A worthless whore like yourself isn't worth anymore of my time today."

Tessa still stares up at him like an innocent little girl searching desperately for comfort. Roman laughs at her. Tears fall out of Tessa's eyes as Roman's anger slowly drops from his face. He never did like seeing Tessa cry, especially when he is the cause of her sadness. With a warm and fatherly gesture, Roman helps Tessa to her feet and holds her shoulders.

"We'll meet again sweetheart." Roman says softly, wiping away her tears, "But next time, your tears will turn into blood."

Roman lightly kisses Tessa's forehead and gives her a warm hug. Tessa remains in his arms, finding the only comfort she will ever have in her life in his embrace. She clutches him tighter, not wanting him to let her go. Roman holds her tightly and runs his hand soothingly through her hair.

"I am everything you will ever have Tessa." Roman says slowly, "One day, you will realize that you are nothing without me."

Roman pushes her off of him. He walks towards the door to leave the room without another glance in her direction. Tessa watches him go, her tears slowly beginning to start again.

"I love you." Tessa calls out weakly, trying to find some compassion in his soul   Roman ignores her statement, but he does stop moving towards the door.

"By the way." Roman says without turning to look at her, "If you really care about your new man, you'll find him outside with several of my closest friends. Hopefully, he is still alive."

Roman then goes into his wallet and takes out a fifty dollar bill. He crumbles the bill in his hands and throws it leisurely over his shoulder. The bill falls to the floor at Tessa's feet, and just like Roman figures, Tessa reaches down and takes the money. Without another word or glance, Roman leaves the room.

Tessa stands in the room alone, not wanting to leave until she stops crying.

<C>   <E>   <O>

After he had hit Andy over the head with the police baton, Drew and his partner proceeded to beat Andy while he helplessly lay on the asphalt. Eventually two more men, who were hidden in the shadows, join in on the beating as well.

Their instructions are simple; don't kill, or injure Andy in any way. They are to merely hurt him in order to show him exactly who he is dealing with. Roman is a good man, who really didn't want an innocent man's death on his conscious. Hopefully, this beating will serve as a warning, and Andy will take the hint so that Roman won't be forced to kill him next time.

Andy collapses once again, his whole body in tremendous pain. He has been jumped before, but he has never been beaten down like this in his life.

Andy has given up trying to defend himself a long time ago. All he can do now is cover himself up and hope to not be killed. After several more kicks, the men decide to stop battering Andy, opting instead to laugh at his misery. Andy lays out on his back, staring up at them in relief because they have finally stopped hurting him.

"This is the man who is protecting Tessa." One thug snickers.

"He can't even defend himself." Drew adds.

"This isn't the challenge I was expecting." Another thug chuckles.

Andy withers in pain as he watches the faces of the four men glare down at him and laugh. Suddenly the thug's laughter ends as a large shadow washes over Andy. He watches from the floor as a large heavy boot steps into his vision. He can't see the face of the man who is attached to the boot, but he can sense the sadistic smile on his face. The boot lifts itself from the ground and rests itself hard on top of Andy's chest. Andy coughs, nearly having the wind knocked out of him from the impact. A puff of cigar smoke hits Andy's face as the fancy boot in front of him chuckles.

"Pathetic." Roman taunts.

The boot slides slowly off of Andy's chest and Roman walks away, followed by the four men who were battering Andy. The five men enter their cars and drive away, leaving Andy flat on his back on the sidewalk.

Andy is coughing and gagging, relieved that the battering is finally over. He feels Tessa's soft hands touch his face. "Are you okay?" Tessa asks, as she helps him up. With Tessa's help, Andy slowly rises to his feet, but he doesn't answer her question. Tessa sighs and helps him walk home.

Andy notices the bruise on Tessa's face and he hangs his head in shame. He failed to protect her when she needed him the most.

<C>   <E>   <O>

Tessa places another cold towel on Andy's forehead. She has finally finished cleaning the blood off of Andy's face and chest. She runs her hand through his hair to ease his pain, as her other hand rubs his chest gently.

Andy lays flat on his back on his couch, losing himself in Tessa's touch. His pain fades as her fingertips run down his chest. Her skin is so soft, and the caring gaze of her midnight black eyes tells Andy that she is truly concerned about his well being. Once again, Tessa's presence and touch makes him feel calm and peaceful.

"Are you okay?" Tessa whispers softly to him.

"I think so." Andy answers her, weakly but with a hint confidence, "Who were they?"

"Roman's friends." Tessa replies, "I was really concerned when he told me that he had you held hostage outside. I immediately left to save you but I was too late."

"I failed you." Andy tells her, wanting to touch the bruise on her face. His hand never made it though; his arm is too numb to lift itself up.

"You didn't fail me." Tessa replies, "You fought long and hard to keep me safe. You didn't tell them where you live did you?"

"They didn't ask me anything." Andy answers, "They just hit me."

Tessa stands up and clutches herself tightly. She paces around worriedly and turns back to him. "I feel so horrible about what happened to you." Tessa softly says and with plenty of concern, "I was so scarred, and I couldn't even do a lap dance to raise the money to pay you."

"I think we should go to the police." Andy says.

At the mention of calling the police, Tessa's whole demeanor changes for the worse. Andy statement surprises and annoys Tessa all at once. She glares at Andy, wanting to slap him in the face instead of nurturing his wounds.

"What?" Tessa asks in shock.

"I think we should go to the police." Andy repeats.

"We can't go to the police." Tessa snaps.

"But I can't protect you." Andy reasons, "Look at the bruise on your face. They assaulted you."

"If you go to the police they will kill me." Tessa yells.

"No the police protect people." Andy insists, "The police will help us." Andy moves to pick up the receiver of his phone but Tessa grasps his hand to stop him.

"You are doing a fine job of protecting me." Tessa reassures allowing her voice to become more seductive, "The only problem we have is that I can't pay you with cash."

Tessa slithers herself onto Andy's lap, allowing her body to glide on top of his as he stares at her, wondering what her intentions are. Tessa takes his hands and grazes them over her breasts, allowing him to feel them in his hands. She slowly brings his hands down her breast and along her waist. Her body warm heat transfers to his aching body as Andy looks up at her innocent but seductive stare.

"Isn't there another way I can pay you?" Tessa whispers and slightly pouts her lips.

She slowly lays her body down on top of his. Her breasts press down on his chest as he looks at her, motionless and speechless at the same time.

Vampyra kisses him, pressing her lips passionately against his. Andy's eyes open wide with surprise, not expecting her to kiss him. Andy can feel Vampyra's tongue move into his mouth as his hands take control of their own motor functions and hold onto her waist. She runs her hands against his chest, allowing then to slowly drift down to his waist and clutch onto his belt.

"No." Andy says, pulling her off of him. Vampyra sits on his lap, running a hand through her hair and innocently gazing into his eyes.

"You don't have to do this." Andy says to her.

"It's okay." Vampyra whispers, "I want to."

Her voice trails off as her lips travel down his cheek and along his neck. She grasps his right hand and presses it against her chest, while taking his left hand and sliding it along her thigh. Andy's body races with desire, paralyzed by the sexual passion radiating off Vampyra's body.

"No." Andy insists, as Vampyra kisses his neck, "This is wrong. I can't..."

"Shhhhhh." Vampyra whispers into his ear.

She slowly glides her lips down Andy's neck, bringing her face to his chest. She softly slides the tip of her tongue along his chest, her hands traveling with her tongue down his body. Andy breathes hard as he feels Vampyra's tongue

against his waist line. He can hear her slowly
undoing his pants as Andy feels his body submitting
to Vampyra's will. He feels a stiffening sensation
between his legs as he watches Vampyra's teeth
unzip his pants. His mind races with excitement as
he lays his body flat on his couch, feeling Vampyra
slowly reach for his boxers ....

"I have a girlfriend." Andy screams out,
frantically pulling Vampyra off of him.

Vampyra looks at him with a very frustrated
expression on her face. Andy quickly readjusts his
clothing. Vampyra removes herself from his lap
and stands in front of Andy. She shakes her head at
him, her eyes revealing that she thinks that he is an
extremely pitiful human being.

"Her name is Amy." Andy explains, "I love
her so much and she's given me her love too."

"She's not giving you enough of it."
Vampyra rudely replies.

"I can't disappoint her." Andy explains, not
really paying attention to what Vampyra has just
said, "I was supposed to take her..."

OH NO!!!!

Andy's body freezes completely. He turns
to look at the clock on his night table, seeing that it
has just turned 1:30 am. Andy begins to sweat with
worry and he can feel himself beginning to
hyperventilate.

"I was supposed to take her out to dinner
tonight." Andy declares, standing up and pacing, "I
was supposed to meet her 8 pm. Oh God what do I
do?"

"Andy, why did you schedule a date when
you were supposed to help me at the club?"
Vampyra asks.

"This was the only day we could see each other and I forgot. Oh God, I have to call her." Andy says to himself, ignoring Vampyra's comments. He reaches for the phone and picks up the receiver to make the call. Vampyra hangs up the phone before he can dial Amy's number. Andy turns to Vampyra, wondering why she has hung up the phone.

"Don't worry about her." Vampyra whispers, "You have me now."

"I have to call her." Andy insists, "I have to make sure she is okay."

Andy picks up the phone again and Vampyra slams it back down onto the holder.

"Andy I got punched in the face today because of you." Vampyra says, pointing out her bruise, "Your job is to look after me. What am I paying you for?"

"I have to call her." Andy declares, pulling the phone back into his hands. Andy begins to dial and Vampyra watches him in frustration. Thinking quickly, Vampyra grabs the phone cord and pulls it out of the wall, ruining the phone jack in the process. Andy hears the phone go dead in his hands.

"That's enough." Vampyra angrily snaps at Andy, "You listen to me. I have a dangerous crime lord trying to kill me. Your problems with your girlfriend can wait until I'm safe."

"I want to call my…." Andy begins to say.

"You are not calling anyone." Vampyra barks, knocking the phone out of his hand and onto the floor. Andy can feel himself getting frustrated as he watches Vampyra grow angrier.

"Look at you Andy." Vampyra mockingly scolds him, "You are a feeble boy working two dead end jobs with a useless girlfriend and a hopeless life. I am giving your existence some type of purpose by having you protect me. If you take down Roman Castle, you will be able to run this town. Your mediocre presence on this planet actually has some meaning to it now, and it is because of me. You are not calling anyone unless I tell you to. No police, no Amy, no fucking girlfriend, nobody!!! Understand me?"

Andy stares at her in a complete daze. Andy has been battered, ridiculed and mocked plenty of times in his life, but never has he been more insulted then in this very moment. Hearing Vampyra speak about him and Amy in this fashion conjures up a rage deep inside of him that he never knew he possessed. A rush of pure adrenaline runs through his veins and body as he watches Vampyra get into his face and look him in the eye.

"Now this is what we are going to do." Vampyra orders, "Tomorrow we are going back to the club. Roman and his men will no doubt be there to try and finish the job. You are going to...."

"Get out of my house." Andy interrupts coldly.

Vampyra pauses for a moment, completely stunned by his words. "Excuse me?" Vampyra rudely asks him.

"Get out of my house. I'm not helping you anymore." Andy repeats, not believing that he is actually standing up to her.

Vampyra laughs at Andy. Andy's stance remains firm and strong, with his eyes locked onto hers. "You can't throw me out." Vampyra laughs, "That isn't apart of the plan."

"It is apart of my plan." Andy states, "I was brutally attacked up by people who I don't even know for you and you don't seem to care."

"I got punched in the…" Vampyra snaps back.

"I got assaulted and battered." Andy yells, "I probably have a broken rib."

"Oh please." Vampyra nastily replies, "You are acting like a child. Now listen to me, we are…."

"No you listen to me." Andy yells, "I have given up three days of my life for you and all that I have gotten in return was getting nearly killed by a gang of criminals."

"You would have gotten your money if you weren't stupid enough to go outside and get caught." Vampyra snaps, "And If you weren't such a prude, I would have at least…."

"I don't want your money or your body." Andy replies, "I just want you out of my house."

Andy feels a great strength soar through his soul. Vampyra gazes at him, still with a dominant smirk on her face. Vampyra can tell by the look in his eyes that he is surprised that he is actually standing up to her. They stare each other down for a few moments until Vampyra laughs.

"You do realize that they will still come after you, even if I'm not here." Vampyra states with a smile, "They will hunt you down until you give up and turn yourself in, just so that Roman will go easy on you when he decides to kill you."

"I'll take my chances." Andy replies confidently.

Vampyra laughs, grabbing her suitcase and her jacket. She puts on her jacket and turns toward the door. Andy keeps staring at her as she opens the door and places her suitcase out of his apartment. She looks back at him and smiles, her expression still unchanged and unintimidated.

"It was fun while it lasted Andy." Vampyra mocks, "Next time, have your little episode after the climax. At least you would have gotten an orgasm out of the deal."

Vampyra leaves Andy's apartment. Never has Andy felt more proud in his life. The adrenaline and confidence running through his nerves makes him feel stronger than he has ever been before. This is the first time Andy ever truly took a stand for what he believed in, and having done so made him wonder why he had never done it before. Andy has fought and won the battle to get his life back, and with Tessa gone, he knew what he had to do first.

Andy sits down on the couch and reaches for the phone to call Amy. It doesn't take long for him to remember that the phone cord has been ripped out of the wall. Andy drops the phone and checks his wallet for money. When he sees that his wallet is empty, he puts it back in his pocket and begins to check his couch cushions for loose change. Despite his search, Andy finds no money anywhere in his apartment.

Andy falls back onto his couch in desperation, breathing heavily as he feels the pain in his chest increasing. His rush of adrenaline has finally died down, slowly being replaced with pain from the beating he has suffered. He grasps his chest to calm himself down, praying to God that he isn't seriously injured.

Just in case you may have forgotten, neither Metal Parts Depot or Moore's Bar and Grill provide medical insurance to their workers.

He spends the rest of the night staring into the ceiling and gripping his chest while trying to will all of his pain away.

CHAPTER 7

Amy spent the whole night crying. She stood outside of the restaurant until 10 pm waiting for Andy and he never showed up. When Amy got to back to the dorm, Megan immediately noticed the sadness in Amy eyes and quickly wrapped her arms around her to comfort her friend.

Amy can't get herself to sleep, the sadness she is feeling is too much to allow her to relax. She had called Andy all night, but he hasn't once picked up his phone. Amy felt that, just like the image of their romantic night, her relationship with Andy has been completely shattered in front of her.

Megan has finally gotten Amy to stop crying, as well as stop calling Andy. She and Amy are now on Amy's bed. Amy is laying down, facing the wall and Megan is sitting on the other side of the bed rubbing Amy's shoulder reassuringly.

"There is a logical explanation for this." Megan nurtures Amy, "Andy probably had to go to work. You know he works all the time and doesn't have a cell phone."

"He would have called me." Amy replies about to cry again, "He would have said something if he remembered me."

"Andy didn't forget about you." Megan says, "He cares about you more than anything and you know that. Something had to have happened to him."

"He has been so busy for the past few months, he must think I'm not important to him anymore." Amy cries.

"You will always be important to him." Megan says. Megan's eyes widen, an idea forming in her head. Megan quickly rises from the bed, turns to Amy and says "Come on get up."

Amy looks up at Megan, confused about what Megan's intentions are. "What are you doing?" Amy sniffles.

"We are going to find out why Andy wasn't there." Megan replies confidently.

"How?" Amy asks.

"We are going to his house today to find him." Megan says. She grabs her bus map and turns back over to Amy and says "Hurry up and get ready. If he isn't home when we get there, we will wait until he comes back."

"What if he doesn't want to see me?" Amy asks, trying to stop crying.

"We will make him see you." Megan says with a smile, "Now hurry up, you and Andy will see each other whether this town wants it to happen or not."

Amy washes her face and changes her clothes. After they are both ready, Megan and Amy leave their dorm to see Andy.

<C>   <E>   <O>

Andy woke up early in the morning, the pain in his chest blistering his body. He felt a little better, but his body is still very bruised from the beating he had taken last night. He manages to get himself ready to go to the warehouse and work. In his current condition, he has no idea how he is going to lift boxes of damaged machinery on and off of lifts, but he has to manage.

Life has to go on.

Andy arrives to work on time. He enters the warehouse, noticing that the other workers are all starring oddly at him. Andy walks through the crowd nervously, wondering why everyone's eyes are focused on him. He approaches the time clock in order to start his day.

Before Andy can clock in, his boss marches towards him. His boss asks him, in a very angry tone, why he had come into work today if he was taking care of a sick mother in the hospital? Andy tries to respond, but can't think of anything to say.

He can't tell his boss that he was told a lie by an exotic dancer who was staying in his apartment.

Andy's hesitation makes his boss angrier. The man humiliates Andy in the middle of the warehouse, berating him with insults before firing him on the spot. Andy asks for forgiveness and begs for his job back, but the boss shows him absolutely no forgiveness.

There is no forgiveness in Windwill Town.

Security immediately grabs Andy and throws him out of the building. Andy lands hard on his chest, feeling a sharp pain run through his body as he turns onto his back to try and relieve the pain.

Andy breathes slowly, trying to gain energy and a normal breathing pattern. He laid out on the sidewalk, trying to will himself up from the ground. Mentally, he is distraught over losing his job and physically, his body is in agony from the beating he had suffered. He tries not to think about his troubles, willing himself harder to rise up from the sidewalk.

He finally stands up, and he starts knocking on the door of the depot in desperation. He is asking anyone, anyone at all, to open the door for him to let him in. He is asking for mercy and forgiveness and searching for human compassion.

No one inside the depot listens to his prays, nobody cares about his cries for help.

Finally giving up on being allowed back into the depot, Andy decides to head for the train. He pushes himself forward, but his legs are moving slower with each step. Andy can feel his whole body ready to give out, so he does all he can to push himself forward.

He falls unconscious on the sidewalk halfway to the train station.

<C>   <E>   <O>

Vampyra slowly walks up the stairs toward Andy's apartment, shuffling through her keys. She knew that she had copied Andy's apartment key a few days ago, all she has to do is find out where she put it.

Vampyra went back to her loft when she left Andy's apartment. When she got there, she had found the place ransacked once again. Roman probably entered her loft after leaving the strip club and tore it apart. Roman destroyed a great deal of her belongings, but Vampyra knows for sure that Roman didn't get what he is looking for.

She is sure of that because Vampyra knows that she doesn't have it.

Andy does.

Vampyra is breaking into Andy's apartment in order to find the box that she had given him at Stalloni's. Having that box is the one way she is able to have Roman, and she didn't want to lose that power.

Vampyra finds the key and places it in the lock to open the door. She steps slowly into the apartment, checking to see if Andy is home. He isn't there, and Vampyra smiles at her own fortune.

"Excuse me, what are you doing?"

Vampyra turns around to see two women standing in front of her. She finds it odd that two attractive looking women are so interested in Andy's apartment, but she decides to play along with them for her own amusement. Vampyra slowly closes and locks the door and then smiles at the two women. She maintains an innocent face as the two women stare at her curiously.

"Who are you and what are you doing in Andy's apartment?" A brunette asks Vampyra. This woman is speaking very strongly and confidently to Vampyra, a quality that admires Vampyra admires in a woman.

Vampyra smiles. "How do you know Andy?" Vampyra asks innocently, "He's never mentioned you before."

"You don't have to know that." The brunette answers. The other girl is staring at Vampyra, very nervous and confused and remaining very close to her friend for support. These are two emotions that Vampyra enjoys to prey on, especially when found in women.

"I'll ask again." The brunette demands, "Who are you and what are you doing here?"

"I'm Andy's girlfriend Tessa." Vampyra answers taking a playful bow, "He asked me pick up something for him in his apartment."

At the mention of the word girlfriend, the two women's eyes widen. The woman who has yet to speak is obviously saddened by Vampyra's words. The brunette looks at her friend and then back at Vampyra with a stern gaze. Vampyra smiles, knowing instantly who the upset girl must be. She just hoped that she can remember her name.

"You must be Amy." Vampyra mockingly greets Amy, "Wow, Andy has told me so much about you."

Amy doesn't answer her, but is shocked to hear Vampyra speak her name. Megan glares at Vampyra, hiding the fact that she is shocked to hear Vampyra's words as well. "Did he tell you that Amy is the woman he loves and his real girlfriend?" Megan challenges.

"Oh he told me a lot about Amy." Vampyra smiles at Megan, "He told me that Amy can never pleasure him the way I do. He also said that he loves the way my body tastes against his lips when we are making love." Amy's eyes widen more and fills with tears as Megan stands firmly in front of Vampyra.

"You're lying. I know you are." Megan snaps defensively, "Andy won't cheat on Amy."

"He's not cheating, he's moving on." Vampyra taunts, in a matter of fact tone, "Amy over there hasn't been apart of his life for such a long time, so Andy went out and got a real woman." Vampyra poses for Amy, showing Amy a rock hard and curvy figure that is far more attractive than Amy's body. Amy starts to cry as Megan holds her friend in her arms.

"Andy and I were together last night." Vampyra tells the two women, licking her lips while reliving her last orgasm in her head, "Just the memory of his large, thick cock between my legs as I grinded him makes me orgasm all over again."

Amy's tears are streaming down her face. Megan turns back to Vampyra with courage in her eyes. "You're lying bitch." Megan challenges angrily. Vampyra is very surprised at Megan's strength and courage. Any other woman, and any man as well, would be putty in Vampyra's hands by now.

"If I'm lying than why was he fucking me last night instead of going out with his so called girlfriend as planned?" Vampyra challenges Megan. Megan's eyes widen at Vampyra's knowledge of Amy and Andy's scheduled date. Amy is shocked as well, which only creates more tears in her eyes.

Vampyra smirks, she definitely has them going.

"Don't blame him for not answering the phone." Vampyra continues, "He couldn't hear it ring over the volume of my moans of pleasure as he pounded his cock between legs."

Amy's tears are flooding the hallway as Vampyra begins running her hands over her body, remembering the feeling of the last time she had sex. Megan balls up her fists, her knuckles turning white with rage as she glares at Vampyra.

"Don't worry honey." Vampyra taunts Amy, "He did think about you that night. I let him call out your name while he was fucking up the ass."

Megan punches Vampyra in the face, no longer able to hold back her hands anymore. Amy runs down the stairs crying, unable to hold back her tears. Vampyra collects herself, surprised by the strength behind Megan's punch. Megan stands tall in front of Vampyra and looks her directly in the eye. Vampyra straightens up as well, the playfulness in her eyes fading to a very serious gaze when she steps right up to Megan's face. The two stare each other down as Vampyra smiles.

"Where is Andy?" Megan demands.

"Buying condoms for our date tonight." Vampyra snickers. Vampyra pushes past Megan and heads downstairs. Megan remains where she is, her head turning so that she can watch Vampyra leave. Vampyra turns back to her as well and give Megan a sinister grin.

"Say goodbye to Amy for me." Vampyra smirks, "Ciao baby."

Vampyra leaves, walking downstairs with a huge smile on her face. That was so much fun, until she got punched in the face. Vampyra holds her head up proudly as she leaves the apartment building, feeling the need to celebrate the damage she has just caused.

She'll come back tonight to find the small box.

<C>   <E>   <O>

Megan finds Amy sitting on the steps between the fourth and fifth floors. Her face is buried in her shirt sleeve and she is crying heavily. Her tears are soaking her clothes as Megan wraps her arms around her friend and kisses her forehead. Amy looks up at Megan, her face red from crying so much.

"How can he do this to me?" Amy cries, "How can he cheat on me?"

"Tessa is lying." Megan confidently declares, "There is something wrong with Andy and Tessa is involved. Do you recognize her at all?"

"I've never seen her before." Amy whimpers, "Andy must have met her at work or some where else..."

"We have to find out who she is and what she is doing to Andy." Megan declares.

"She is so much more attractive than I am." Amy cries, "What guy wouldn't take her over me?"

Megan grabs her friend and looks her in the eye with compassion. "Andy is not cheating on you." Megan states, "And I'm going to prove it. Do you know where Tony is right now?"

"Probably at home or work." Amy answers.

"Let's talk to Tony and see if he knows something." Megan suggests, helping Amy up, "Come on let's go. We have to help Andy."

Megan and Amy leave the apartment building.

<C>　　<E>　　<O>

Andy wakes up in front of The Metal Parts Depot. He has no idea how long he has been unconscious, but by the change in the sun, he was probably out for a few hours. There were people on the street who saw Andy laying out on the pavement during that time, but nobody lifted a finger to help him up. Some people did take the time to stop and rob him though, stealing his bag with his restaurant uniform inside of it and the watch that Amy gave him for his birthday a year ago, but nobody was interested in helping him up.

In Windwill Town, there is no respect for your fellow man.

When Andy finally rises, he makes his way to the train station. Andy sees the homeless man who lives in the station glaring at him with laughter in his eyes. The homeless man is drinking a bottle of soda, and even though it hadn't once belonged to Andy, the homeless man is mocking him with the refreshing liquid. There is a half eaten candy bar in the man's other hand, which he uses to give himself a toast before drinking some soda.

Even the homeless are better off than Andy

Andy slowly makes his way onto the train to go to Moore's Bar and Grill for the first time in the last three days. He has no uniform, and no food to fill his stomach. He sits on the train and looks up at the roof, praying that he isn't too late.

<C>   <E>   <O>

Andy stumbles up to Moore's Bar and Grill, in pain but ready for his shift. He gathers himself, trying to look as presentable as possible for work. He enters the restaurant, trying to mask the frustration, exhaustion and pain of the day from his face and body language.

He didn't make it pass the front counter.

Andy's general manager stops him and asks him why he hadn't come to work for the last three days. Andy hesitates for several moments, trying to think of what to say. As the moments of silence tick away, Andy's boss gets more impatient for a response.

Andy doesn't even get the chance to speak before the manager harshly scolds him for not coming to work. The manager dehumanizes Andy in front of the store and its customers with his words and slaps to the face. Then to top things off, he punches Andy in his face and happily yells out the words he has wanted to say to Andy for so many years.

"YOU'RE FIRED!!!!!!!!!"

Andy pleads with his manager to not fire him. Andy explains that he has to pay his rent.

Andy explains that he has just been fired from his other job and really needs the income. Andy gets down on his hands and knees and begs his manager to give him another chance.

The manager grabs his crotch and tells Andy to suck his dick for his job back. Andy hangs his head low in shame, not knowing what else to say. The manager laughs at Andy's embarrassment and walks away from him, returning to the kitchen area to continue his shift.

Andy finally rises as he hears and watches several people in the restaurant laugh at him. His coworkers look at him sympathetically, wishing that there is something they can do to help a man who isn't that much different from them. They are all a group of innocent people, working very hard just to survive in the cruel and harsh world. Andy finally reaches the front door, wanting to escape the humiliation as soon as he possible. Andy grabs the door knob to walk out the door.

"Oh Andy, I forgot something." The manager calls out.

Andy turns back to the kitchen wondering what more he will have to endure. The manager is standing at the front counter menacingly waving Andy's check in front of him. Andy's eyes widen with hope as his body instinctively turns him around to take his money. Before Andy can take one step, the manager rips Andy's last paycheck to pieces, throwing the newly formed confetti into the air above him in victory.

Andy's hopes crumble as the tiny pieces of his paycheck hit the ground of the restaurant. The manager laughs out loud and so do several customers sitting in the dinner. The crew watches the sight with great sadness and sympathy for Andy Combs.

Without another word, Andy leaves Moore's Bar and Grill for the last time. The only thing left to do now is to go home and figure out what he will do next.

<C>   <E>   <O>

After leaving Andy's apartment, Megan and Amy call Tony to figure out where he is. Tony picks up his phone, and Megan tells him what is going on. After hearing the story, Tony invites Megan and Amy to his apartment son that they can discuss the situation together. The two women head Tony's apartment and Megan repeats the story once again.

Tony is sitting on his couch with a look of complete bewilderment. Megan is sitting on a chair on the left side of Tony's couch, also thinking about what to make of Tessa. Amy paces around the room, hoping to find the answer to her question on Tony walls.

"It doesn't make sense." Tony exclaims, "I spoke to Andy the night before and he seemed okay to me."

"There has to be something wrong Tony." Megan insists, "Andy won't cheat on Amy, but this Tessa woman has keys to Andy's apartment. Does Andy have a female landlord?"

"No." Tony replies, "Andy's landlord is a fat greasy waste of life."

"Then who is Tessa?" Megan asks.

"Landlord's daughter?" Tony suggests, but not believing it himself, "Did you try calling Andy?"

"We already called plenty of times and his phone isn't working. We can't get him at work because he doesn't have a cell phone." Megan says, "Why don't we catch him between jobs and talk to him?"

Tony checks the time before responding. "He should already be working in Moore's Bar and Grill. We can wait outside for him, he'll be done at around 1 am."

Megan and Tony continue to debate as Amy wanders around Tony's apartment. Amy has so many questions and she is so confused that she can't get herself to sit down and relax. She has to keep moving so that she can occupy her mind with different thoughts other than the painful ones she is experiencing now.

Is Andy really cheating on me?

Who is Tessa?

Why does she have keys to his apartment?

Why did he skip out on our date?

These questions race through her mind before she can actually answer them. Realistically though, it isn't like she actually has the answers to these questions to begin with.

Tessa's image is into her memory. Tessa's hair is midnight black and silky, putting Amy's hair to shame. Tessa's natural breasts are at least two cup sizes bigger than Amy's and they are also rounder and firmer as well. Tessa's legs and body are more sculpted and toned than Amy's body. Tessa's skin is softer than Amy's.

And in terms of pleasuring a man, Tessa can obviously perform much better and longer than Amy.

What man will choose Amy when they can be with a woman like Tessa?

Amy lowers her head in shame as images of Tessa and Andy sleeping together flood her mind. She looks down onto Tony's desk in shame, seeing Tessa's amazing body clothed in tight black leather lingerie. Her hair flows like a lustful wind that flows into the room. She sees Tessa on her hands and knees on a stage as Andy calls out her name....
VAMPYRA AT FANTASIA'S SURRENDER

What!!!!

Amy picks up a postcard from Tony's desk that shows Tessa on her hands and knees on a stage. It is a postcard advertising Vampyra's show at Fantasia's Surrender. Amy looks anxiously at the postcard, her whole body becoming screaming out with discovery as her mind races to try and get her to produce the words.

"I found her." Amy gasps.

Tony and Megan's conversation ends when they hear Amy's sudden words. They turn to Amy, wondering what she has discovered. Amy eagerly runs to her friends, with the postcard in her hands. "I found her." Amy repeats, but clearer so that she can be heard. Amy stands in front of her friends, showing Tony and Megan the postcard. Megan takes the postcard from Amy and looks at it in complete shock.

"She's right. This is Tessa, this is her." Megan exclaims, giving the postcard to Tony.

"Vampyra." Tony says in disbelief, "She's a dancer at Fantasia's Surrender. Andy and I saw her a few days ago when I took him to the club."

"Andy went to a strip club." Amy asks with jealously.

"Did you talk to her?" Megan asks, "Or exchange numbers or something?"

"No." Tony answers defensively, "We just watched her dance and that's all."

Amy and Megan see Tony getting slightly nervousness.

"Andy didn't do anything, promise." Tony assures, "He was a gentleman the whole night. We just watched that's all."

"That's her." Amy insists, "Andy had to have gotten in contact with her some how."

"All she did was dance and leave." Tony tells them, "She was gone before anyone could approach her." Megan stands up from the couch and throws on her coat. She turns back to Tony and Amy.

"I say we go there and figure out what's going on." Megan suggests, "Are you up for this Amy?"

"Of course." Amy answers.

"Then let's go." Tony firmly states.

The three friends leave Tony's apartment and towards Fantasia's Surrender to find answers.

<C>   <E>   <O>

Amy has never been to a strip club before so she has no idea what to expect. Watching women on a small stage dancing with barely any clothes on made Amy very uncomfortable and nervous. She can see some of the men staring at her and Megan too, expecting them to hit the stage and dance as well. Their hunger for her made her want to walk out of the club as soon as possible and bath all of their impurities off of her.

Megan is strong enough to not pay them any mind, a quality that Amy is finds very admirable about her best friend. Tony stands close to Amy and takes her hand in order to comfort her. He knows that she is terrified and he hopes that maybe if the men think that he is Amy's boyfriend they will leave her alone.

It didn't help at all.

They just think that he is her pimp.

Amy and Megan take a seat while Tony walks the floor to ask some of the dancers and guards about Vampyra. The guards tell him to wait until she gets on stage while the women offer him a lap dance to forget about Vampyra. Tony returns to Amy and Megan with no information. They develop a plan, deciding that Tony will ask Vampyra for a lap dance when she leaves the stage. Megan and Amy will enter the room with them to corner Vampyra and then they will get their answers.

Also visiting Fantasia's Surrender tonight is Roman Castle's most trusted associate Drew. Drew is also waiting for Vampyra, and while sitting in the club, he has taken notice of Tony's search for her. It isn't everyday that a man asks about Vampyra as innocently as Tony is, and since Drew doesn't recognize him, there is a good chance that this man is seeking something other than a lap dance from Roman's little Tessa. Drew puts on his dark sunglasses and casually leaves his table and approaches Tony.

"Excuse me." Drew says to Tony after tapping him on the shoulder, "I couldn't help but overhear that you are looking for a woman named Vampyra. Is this correct?"

The three friends turn towards Drew, and none of them answer him right away. Megan and Tony are eyeing him curiously, sizing up who this man is and trying to see if they can trust him. Amy also wonders who is, and whether or not he can answer her all questions.

"We're looking for Vampyra." Tony answers, "Do you know where she is?"

"I'm curious to know why you are looking for her." Drew answers, his stone faced expression remaining unchanged.

"How about you tell us why you want to know and we'll tell you why we're looking for her?" Megan asks with a challenging glare in her eyes.

Drew smirks at Megan's gaze, appreciating the fact that this woman is standing up to him. "Okay beautiful, I'll tell you." Drew says while removing his sunglasses, "My name is Drew. I'm looking for Vamprya because she has taken something very valuable from my employer and is hiding it in a man's home."

Drew pauses for a moment to allow his story to settle with them. "Now, why are you looking for Vampyra?" Drew asks.

Amy, Megan and Tony look at Drew determining whether he is actually telling the truth. Drew watches them as well, determining their interest in Vampyra on his own. He has a hunch, and it will not hurt to test it out and see what the end result is.

"Perhaps you know this man?" Drew suggests, his voice and emotions remaining unchanged. Drew takes out a photo of Andy and the three friends look at it and then at each other.

"That's Andy." Amy says in surprise, "Why are you looking for Andy?"

"Hold on a second." Tony says, "Andy doesn't have the time to protect Vampyra. Andy works two jobs and….."

"Your friend Andy has been seen in this club with Vampyra for the past three days and we have spotted him with Vampyra during the day as well." Drew informs. Drew takes out more photos to prove his statement and shows them to the three friends.

"No it can't be." Amy says, "Andy wouldn't steal anything or even hide stolen belongings. Andy is a good man."

"Well your friend Andy is charged by my employer for theft and aiding a criminal." Drew explains, "If you tell me why you are here, perhaps your testimony can clear his name."

"How can we trust you?" Megan asks, "Who is your employer?"

"If Andy's name isn't cleared, and my men find him, he will be punished." Drew states, "I wouldn't want to watch an innocent man face a brutal punishment for no reason."

Megan and Tony remain cautious, but Amy's eyes glow with fright. She can't bear the thought of Andy getting arrested and sent to jail. The streets of Windwill Town are bad enough, having to go to jail in Windwill Town will be allot worse. She is convinced that Andy has done nothing wrong, and must do everything in her power to keep Andy out of harm's way.

"We'll go with you." Amy instantly tells Drew. Drew smiles as Megan and Tony look at Amy in disbelief. Amy looks back at her friends, wondering why they are not in agreement with her decision.

"We have to talk for a second." Tony says to Drew. Megan and Tony pull Amy to the side, far enough away from Drew so that he can't hear their conversation. Drew stands confidently, his expression and body language unchanged, as he watches the three friends talk.

"Are you crazy Amy?" Megan whispers, "That man is a mobster. I don't know why he has Andy's picture, but you can't trust anything this guy says."

"Andy is in trouble Megan and we have to help him." Amy insists, "If this mobster has Andy's picture, he is in even more danger than we thought."

"We should wait until we can talk to Vampyra and see what is going on." Tony suggests, "We can clear this all up right here. It will be safer for everyone."

"I can't let anything happen to Andy." Amy says, "We can keep Andy out of trouble by just telling these people that Andy didn't do anything."

"Amy, it doesn't work that way." Megan insists, "I know what kind of people they are Amy; I've been around them and I've lived with them all my life remember. He will kill us all if we trust him."

"He is the only man who can help us." Amy insists, "If you guys want to stay here and try to find Vampyra you can, but I'm going to keep these people from hurting Andy."

Amy pushes past Megan and Tony and walks over to Drew. Amy and Drew exchange words and then Amy turns to Megan and Tony. Amy has made up her mind, and regardless of whether Megan and Tony go with her, she is leaving the club with Drew tonight. The two friends look at Amy and, despite their gut feelings, walk over to Amy and join her and Drew.

They can't let Amy go into the mob alone.

Drew and the three friends leave Fantasia's Surrender in Drew's car and head towards Roman's mansion. The rest of Drew's team, who are all unseen by the three friends, stay at the club with orders to kill Andy upon sight.

<C>   <E>   <O>

Drew guides Tony, Megan and Amy to Roman's office. Drew had informed Roman of their arrival, during the ride to the mansion. He could sense how pleased Roman was at Drew's discovery of Andy's friends. Roman wants Andy dead, whether or not he has taken Roman's hint, and anyway he can get closer to Andy he will take.

If it is a game Tessa wants, then it is a game she will get.

Drew stands in front of Roman's office door and turns to the three friends. Megan and Tony are looking around very cautiously, still feeling wary about entering Roman's mansion. Amy is fearful of Andy's fate and eager to approach Roman Castle and explain to him that Andy is innocent.

"Roman Castle is in his office." Drew says, "If you want to clear Andy's name, he is the man to convince."

"Let us in then." Megan says, clearly not liking the situation. Drew smiles at Megan, and opens the door for them. Megan can sense him undressing her with his eyes as she, Tony and Amy walk into the office.

Megan couldn't be happier when the door closes behind her and she is out of Drew's sight. Roman's office is eerily silent and still, the only movement in the room coming from small bursts of cigar smoke coming from the desk chair. Roman is sitting in this chair with his back turned to the three friends. Roman's mysteriousness and secrecy have only made Megan and Tony even more cautious of their surroundings, neither one finding any reason to trust anything around them.

"Are you Roman Castle?" Tony asks.

"I am." Roman replies, without turning the chair around, "Now, can I ask who you are?"

"I'm Amy, Andy's girlfriend." Amy answers quickly, "I came here to tell you that Andy didn't do anything wrong. That stripper is the one who stole from you. Andy would never do anything like that."

"Andy is harboring stolen goods and the criminal who robbed me in his home." Roman replies in a matter of fact tone, "That makes him an accomplice to the crime."

"Andy isn't a criminal, he is a good and honest men." Amy says.

"Then how come he hasn't gone to the police?" Roman asks.

"That stripper has to be threatening his life with something." Amy tries to reason, "Andy is a good man."

"The more you say that the more you lessen it's meaning." Roman replies coldly.

Amy is about to respond but Tony stops her. "My name is Tony sir." Tony says, "I don't know what connection Andy has with Vampyra, but I can guarantee you that Andy is in no way apart of any criminal actions taken by that stripper."

"SHE IS NOT THAT STRIPPER!!!!!!." Roman barks, swinging his chair around and angrily rising out of it to face the three friends. There is an awkward silence in the room. Amy, Tony and Megan are all equally surprised by Roman's sudden outburst. Roman composes himself and puts out his cigar.

"I don't like it when someone refers to my sweet Tessa as that stripper." Roman says.

Tony, Megan and Amy look at him unsure of what to say. Roman walks over to the three friends. "You are chasing an enemy that you know nothing about." Roman explains, "Would you like to know who Vampyra really is?"

The three friends nod.

Roman tells his story....

Tessa is the birth daughter of a 17 year old girl who was gang rapped in an alley somewhere around the housing project district of Windwill Town. Anyone of the five men who rapped this honest high school graduate that night can be Tessa's father, but since none of them were ever caught, no one ever will know.

Tessa's mother named Tessa after her mother, who died while trying to save her daughter from being rapped. Tessa's mother and her older brother lived in their small apartment with baby Tessa for two years before the Windwill Town Social Services Office pulled the child out of the home and into a shelter. The heart broken mother desperately fought to get her daughter back, but she simply didn't have the money or the power to fight the system. Tessa's mother never had any further contact with her baby after that day.

Tessa remained in the dirty and poorly managed orphanage for another seven years, going from foster home to foster home. With every home Tessa went to, she would create so much trouble that the foster parents will take her back to the orphanage. Finally, Tessa had enough of living in an orphanage all her life. She finally ran away, seeking her on independence and not wanting to rely on anyone else.

Tessa lived on the streets, surviving by pick pocketing and lock picking for three years until one day, she successfully completed the greatest pick pocket of her life.

She pick pocketed Roman Castle on a street corner while he was surrounded by his body guards. His guards realized this and chased the 11 year old down. They caught her and immediately tried to kill her before Roman Castle stopped them and took the girl by the hand. He took Tessa to his mansion, commending her for her stealth and strength. He gave Tessa a room in his large mansion and raised her as if she were his very own flesh and blood. He also showed her his various businesses and improved her skills of thievry and manipulation.

Roman has always seen something in Tessa that reminded him of himself when he was a child. He hopes that she will follow in his footsteps to greatest and immortality in Windwill Town and become the most powerful woman in Windwill Town.

As Tessa went through puberty, Roman became very protective of his beautiful surrogate daughter. Her body developed early, and grew more beautiful by the day, making it hard for Roman's henchmen to not take notice of her. His henchmen tried to gain her affections on more than one occasion and Roman became very jealous and angry towards the attention that his little Tessa was receiving.

Tessa flirted a great deal with his staff, but there is only one man who Tessa's desire and lust belongs to. Tessa is in love, and will always be in love with Roman Castle. Tessa is drawn to him by his strong and masculine appearance as well as his success and power. Even though he is like a father to her, Tessa wanted nothing more than to give herself to Roman as she has witnessed other women do in the past.

One night, when Roman was scolding his 17 year old daughter for being too flirtatious with his staff, Tessa admitted her undying desire for him and she offered herself to him. Roman was surprised at first, but in her nightgown and with her lips pursed he no longer saw her as his daughter. Roman took her that night, giving Tessa the most wonderful experience she has ever had in her life.

After that night, Tessa's body urged for more experience and pleasure. Tessa flirted more and more with the staff until she started sleeping with them. Roman grew angrier as he started catching his daughter with his hired guns on several occasions. Tessa enjoyed watching Roman's jealousy grow, so much so that it turned her on and influenced her to make him angrier as the days went by. Eventually, she stopped hiding her short affairs around the house so it would be easier for Roman to catch her in the act.

Roman would murder his henchman and furiously scold and beat Tessa, until he would finally calm down and then eventually have sex with her once again to wipe her tears away. Roman's businesses started dwindling as he lost more henchmen and business partners to Tessa's seduction. As Roman's businesses dwindled, Roman's massive wealth would decrease as well.

The cycle continued for several years until Roman's mind reached it's limit of frustration and jealously and Tessa's emotions became overwhelmed with anger and misery. Roman didn't want any other man touching his little Tessa, and he also didn't want Tessa around to ruin his wealth and tempt his men. Tessa was tired of Roman's beatings and rules and longed her own independence.

Even though neither one of them wanted the other around, neither Tessa nor Roman could stand the thought of not being apart of each other's life.

One day, after Roman beat a man to death in front of Tessa because he was caught in bed with her, Roman and Tessa sat down and discussed how they could both be free from their torment. Roman bought Tessa her own loft far from his mansion, and told Tessa that he would provide everything for her that she will ever need in her entire life, just as long as she stays away from his home, his henchmen, all of his associates and business partners, and more importantly, Roman Castle himself for the rest of her life. Tessa agreed, and that night, they shared their last night of passion before they will never see each other again.

Bright and early the next day, Tessa moved out of Roman's mansion and moved into her luxury loft on the border of Harold's Square. The apartment came fully furnished, stock with all of Tessa's favorite food and with closets filled with a large designer wardrobe. Tessa enjoyed her brand new home, and celebrated by going on a shopping spree with Roman's credit card.

Roman's businesses flourished again, his power, influence and money growing greater than ever before. While Roman's life expanded, Tessa's life became completely dependant on Roman's money. Roman saw to it that Tessa would never have anything unless he gave it to her, and he used his spies to follow her twenty four / seven to make sure that Tessa remained nothing without him.

This isn't the independence that Tessa had in mind.

Recently, Tessa killed all of Roman's spies to escape his hold over her. She then entered Roman's house and stole some of Roman's valuables so that she can pawn them to build a life of her own.

Also, she took the job as a dancer for Fantasia's surrender in order to prove that she can make money on her own.

So their relationship is very much like a double edged sword. Both of them have absolute happiness in each other's presence. However, both of them will feel nothing but misery as long as they are together.

This is the real story of Tessa and Roman's relationship, and of course, a much less violent, sexual, and Roman friendly story was told to Tony, Amy and Megan.

"Tessa stole plenty of my belongings and sold them all but one." Roman explains, "I want Tessa and my belongings back in my custody. Your friend Andy is holding her in his apartment. If I have to, I will kill him to get to her."

"You can't hurt Andy." Amy begs, "He is innocent, I swear, he won't do anything to harm you."

"Than inform your friend to turn Tessa in to me at once and he will be cleared of all charges." Roman says very emotionlessly.

"We'll tell him, as soon as we can find him." Amy says, "His phone is disconnected and he...."

"So he is trying to run away?" Roman asks.

Amy is about to speak and Megan stops her. "Why don't we get your stuff and give it to you?"

Megan suggests, "Just tell us what it is and we will go to Andy's apartment and get it for you. That way, you will have your stuff and Andy is clear of all of his charges."

Roman smiles and walks up to the three friends. "Excellent idea." Roman laughs, "But you're not going alone. My driver and I will accompany you to his apartment so that I can guarantee that my belongings are returned to me."

"You're not going anywhere near Andy's apartment." Megan firmly states, "You can trust us. We'll get you your stuff."

"How do I know that I can trust you?" Roman asks, "You claim to be his good friends, you three could be in on this scam with him."

"We have nothing against you, we just want Andy to be protected and his name cleared." Tony states.

"Then you will have no problem allowing me to accompany you to Andy's apartment in order to retrieve my belongings." Roman states, "As far as I'm concerned, you have no choice but to accept this offer."

Amy is about to speak but Tony and Megan stop her. Amy turns to them with desperation in her eyes. Tony and Megan walk to a corner of the room that is out of Roman's earshot, dragging Amy behind them. They huddle together to speak privately.

"Let's go." Tony suggests to Amy, "We aren't going to allow this man in Andy's apartment."

"This is the only way we can save Andy." Amy pleads, "He won't hurt Andy if he has his stuff back."

"Amy you're talking about allowing a mob boss in your boyfriend's apartment." Megan warns, "He could kill Andy upon sight and then kill us to. I heard of Roman Castle, he is one of the deadliest men in Windwill Town. We have to find Andy ourselves and get him somewhere safe."

"Andy can stay with me." Tony suggests, "It will be cramped but he could live with me until we have this sorted out."

"By then Andy could be dead." Amy declares, "We can't just bury Andy in the city and hope they never find him."

Amy pulls away from her friends and turns to Roman. "We accept your offer." Amy says, "I will take you to Andy's apartment right now so that you can retrieve your belongings, but you have to promise that you won't hurt Andy."

"Agreed." Roman says, in a matter of fact tone, "I give you my word that I, nor any of my men, will hurt Andy from this point on, as long as I get my belongings back. To prove my truce, only my driver and I will come along. All my henchmen will remain here at the mansion."

"Agreed." Amy says, turning to her friends and saying, "It's the only way to protect him."

Megan and Tony stare at Amy in disbelief, trying to find a way to undo the deal. It is too late, the deal has been made and there is no turning back from here.

<C>   <E>   <O>

Andy arrives home, finally climbing the last staircase to reach the fifth floor.

He is both physically and mentally exhausted after everything that has happened to him in the last twenty four hours. How has his life come to this? Just last week Andy was working two shitty jobs, getting treated like shit and making shit for money.

Now all he has is shit.

He slumps against his door, trying to think of what he can possibly do to convince his former employers to hire him back. Andy is already struggling with his bills, and a complete lack of income does nothing to help his situation.

Why did he allow Tessa to ruin his life like this? Andy lost everything because of her. It is hard to find any kind of legal work in Windwill Town, how will Andy ever find another job so that he can afford to live? Correction, how can Andy be able to find two jobs so that he can afford to survive?

Andy slowly reaches for his keys to open the door to his apartment. He not only hurt myself, but he has also let Amy down. He loves Amy so much, and he promised her that one day he would marry her and support her the way that she deserved to be living.

Like a knight in shining armor, Andy wants to lift Amy onto his horse and carry her out of Windwill Town and into a prospering city where their children can be raised without fear and hardships. Amy will become a successful nurse at the world's leading hospital, while Andy will become the famous writer that he has dreamed to be. Amy will always be happy because she will have everything she wants and their children will never have to go through anything that their parents had to while growing up.

Amy told Andy once that she doesn't need anything but Andy's love, but Andy didn't see how that would be possible. If Andy can't financially support Amy, how can she be happy? How can Amy have everything she can ever want if Andy doesn't have the money to provide it. By losing all his income, he has failed Amy's love for him and shattered her dreams of a better tomorrow.

Andy doesn't deserve Amy's love and support. Andy doesn't deserve anything anymore.

He places his keys into the lock, and to his surprise, his house keys no longer fit in the keyhole. Andy struggles with his keys, wondering why the door isn't opening as his anxiety and desperation grows on his face. He doesn't even notice Mr. McGuckin's door swing open and his heavy footsteps pound into the hallway.

"Hair Comb you son of a bitch get the fuck over here." Mr. McGuckin growls.

Andy jumps in surprise at Mr. McGuckin's snarling voice. He drops his keys and rushes over to Mr. McGuckin, the desperation and sweat dripping down his face.

"I'm sorry for making so much noise sir." Andy pants, "There is just a problem with my…"

"I changed the locks to your apartment this morning you lying sack of shit." Mr. McGuckin growls.

"Why?" Andy frantically asks.

"I don't know what kind of people raised you Hair Comb." Mr. McGuckin begins, "But here in Windwill town people either pay their rent or they don't have a place to live."

"Sir I…."Andy says.

"That fine piece of ass that you brought into this building a couple days ago promised me hot sex in exchange for your rent money." Mr. McGuckin says, "That whore never came to my room and I haven't seen her or you since!!!!!!"

"Sir.. I…" Andy says.

"I want hot sex Hair Comb!!!!" Mr. McGuckin yells into Andy's face, his horrible breath swimming into Andy's nostrils and making him want to vomit.

"Sir I don't…." Andy says.

"Listen up you rotten piece of crap." Mr. McGuckin yells, "You are not entering that apartment until I receive one of two things from you. I want my five hundred and fifty dollars rent money or that hot curvy slut in my hands right now!!!!!!!"

"Sir I only owe you two hundred…." Andy says.

"FIVE HUNDRED DOLLARS OR THE SLUT!!!!!!!" McGuckin yells, "NOW!!!!!!!!!!!!"

Andy can't fight the tears in his eyes. They stream down his face as Andy feels his knees becoming weak and limb. He doesn't collapse, but his body really wants to. He hangs his head in absolute defeat.

"Sir I just lost my jobs." Andy defeatedly admits, "I have no money to give you, and I won't until I am employed again."

What else can he say?

Mr. McGuckin stares at Andy in surprise and his anger starts to die down. Andy's face becomes more desperate and defeated. Andy gazes at the disgusted Irish man, seeking understanding and forgiveness in his eyes. Mr. McGuckin starts to smile, however, his smile lacks any kind of compassion for Andy's situation.

"You can't pay my rent Hair Comb?" Mr. McGuckin asks slowly and inquisitively.

"No sir." Andy answers lightly, "But tomorrow I will be job hunting and you can have any pay check I receive until your rent is completely paid off. Please sir, I have no where else to go."

Mr. McGuckin smiles even wider as Andy's tears fall faster. He kicks off his right shoe and looks Andy in the eye. "Get down on your knees and beg me to allow you back into that apartment." Mr. McGuckin commands.

Andy's body responds before his mind can even register what McGuckin had told him to do. Andy is on his knees, looking up at Mr. McGuckin and holding his sock. Andy looks into Mr. McGuckin's eyes, looking for sympathy and reason in the man's face. "Please sir." Andy begs, "I have no where else to go. Please."

"Kiss my feet." Mr. McGuckin commands.

Mr. McGuckin's smile becomes overwhelmed with power. Andy's lips fall onto his dirty right sock, kissing it for mercy. McGuckin lets out a loud guttural laugh as he kicks Andy off of his feet to add to Andy's embarrassment. Mr. McGuckin spits in his face and the yellowed wad of flem hits Andy between the eyes. Mr. McGuckin laughs louder and harder than he has ever laughed before.

"You're a useless, sack of shit and bone Hair Comb." Mr. McGuckin laughs. Andy stares up at the man, unable to lift himself off of the ground.

"You have no job, you can't pay my rent and that dirty slut isn't here to fuck me and you think I'm going to allow you in my apartment." Mr. McGuckin says.

"Sir...I..." Andy pleads.

"Shut the fuck you waste of life." Mr. McGuckin yells at Andy and laughs louder, "You can consider yourself evicted from my building."

"But my stuff is in there." Andy pleads, "Please just let me have my stuff."

"Hell no." Mr. McGuckin laughs, "That crap belongs to me now. I'll sell everything in that apartment until your five hundred and fifty dollar bill has been completely paid off."

"Sir, that is all I have." Andy begs, "You can't take....."

"Get the fuck out of my building you worthless piece of scum." Mr. McGuckin growls once again spitting at Andy. Andy scrambles up from the floor, trying to block Mr. McGuckin's flem as he runs down stairs. Andy can hear Mr. McGuckin yelling and laughing as he races down the stairs and out of the apartment complex.

It is raining outside and the streets are very dark and uninviting. Andy stands in front of the apartment building, looking up to see Mr. McGuckin hanging out of his window with crushed beer cans in his hands.

"Get away from my property asshole." Mr. McGuckin screams out into the night as he launches beer cans at Andy. Andy runs, dodging the beer cans as best he can. Andy loses his balance and trips, falling into a large puddle several feet away from the building. Andy's clothes and face are drenched by the rain water, but at least Andy runs out of Mr. McGuckin's range.

Andy lifts himself slowly out of the puddle, the tears on his face still coming down. Andy cries harder as he stumbles through the streets, clutching himself for warmth as the rain drowns him and blinds his walk.

He has nothing now. Andy has lost his jobs, his apartment and everything that he owns because of the foolish idea to try and help someone. With no phone and no money, Andy can't even get himself something to eat, or even call his friends and ask for any kind of help.

All Andy has now is the cold and soaked clothes on his back, the rumbling of his empty stomach, the weakness in his bones and muscles and the luring cloud of failure that is hovering over his spirit.

Out of the corner of his eye, he sees a homeless family watching him from an alley. There is a father, mother, sister and brother surrounding a camp fire built inside of a steel garbage can. Somehow, the little wooden shelter that they have luckily found as refuge for themselves in the alley is enough to protect the flame and house the family from the rain. They all stare at Andy and Andy stares back; defeated tears and rain covering his face.

The family leaves their shelter to surround Andy, taking him by the hand and guiding him over to their wooden shelter. Andy allows himself to be taken into the family's arms. They lay him on top of some old blankets and clothing they have on the floor. The sister and mother kiss Andy lightly on his checks to reassure him and work to make him comfortable. The father and son add some newspaper to the flame to make it stronger and warmer. They place blankets on top of Andy and lay down next to him, their collective warmth keeping Andy warm and cozy.

Eventually the fire goes out and the family and Andy fall asleep inside the wooden shack. It is a small, old and rundown shelter, but somehow it provides much needed warmth, protection and comfort to its occupants.

Sometimes the coldest, darkest street corners can provide more warmth than the largest and brightest buildings.

Yes, there is comfort existing in the hearts of some citizens in Windwill Town; and on this night, and possibly forever, this little wooden shack and homeless family will probably be the only comfort that Andy Combs will ever have.

CHAPTER 8

Amy, Megan and Tony follow Roman down to the garage where all of his luxury cars are kept. Roman has a meeting with his men, informing them that they are no longer allowed to hunt for Andy Combs. His men nod their heads to show their understanding of the command. Roman's end of the deal has been made, and now, it is Amy's turn.

Amy gets into a limo with Roman. Megan and Tony move to the vehicle as well, but Roman stops them. The deal is that Amy and Roman go to Andy's apartment, Megan and Tony aren't invited to join them. So, Megan and Tony unwillingly stay behind as Amy rides off with Roman. The two friends remain silent until the car is completely out of view.

"This isn't a good idea." Megan says in frustration, "She can't trust Roman. She shouldn't be doing this."

"We need to follow them." Tony suggests, "We need to get a car."

Tony and Megan move through the garage and towards one of Roman's black convertibles. The doors are locked, which isn't a problem for Megan, having hijacked many vehicles back in her day. Megan takes a hair pin out of her hair and works on the lock as Tony stands by the convertible, blocking Megan from sight.

"Got it." Megan says, smiling and replacing the hair pin in her hair, "Come on lets go."

Tony grabs the door handle and enters the vehicle. Megan walks over to the passenger side to enter the car. Tony opens the door for her, but Megan doesn't walk into the car. Instead, a man's hand slams the door closed and knocks on the window. Tony slowly steps out of the car to figure out what is going on.

Drew is holding Megan firmly against his chest. He is also holding a knife to her throat. Tony closes the car door and slowly backs away from it as Drew smiles and sniffs Megan's hair.

"What are you doing?" Drew asks as he holds Megan close to him.

"Let her go." Tony demands.

"The deal is that you and her stay here while your friend goes to get my boss's belongings back." Drew says, "Now I'll ask again, what are you doing?"

"We are staying here." Tony answers cautiously, "Now, let her go."

Drew laughs as he places his arm around Megan's waist and brings the knife up closer to her lower jaw. "I can kill her right now and you won't be able to stop me." Drew taunts, holding Megan very tightly and longingly, "But what a waste it would be to hurt someone so beautiful."

"Leave her alone." Tony warns, "Your boss told you not to hurt any of us." Tony's hand slips into his pocket, slowly pulling out the gun he has brought along just in case of an emergency.

"And your friend told you to stay behind." Drew challenges, "As far as I'm concerned, I can do with her what I please as compensation."

"I won't let you." Tony says, whipping his gun hand up and pointing the barrel at Drew. Drew doesn't flinch as Tony clicks a bullet into the barrel. Drew smiles at Tony, sliding his hands along Megan's thigh as he waits for Tony to make a move.

There is a shot, and finally Drew flinches. His hands remain as firm on the knife as possible as more shots are fired in the room. Megan closes her eyes in fear as Drew's grip on her begins to loosen. Tony stares angrily at drew, gripping his gun firmly.

Tony hits the ground, his chest filled with bullet wounds as two more gun shots hit him in the arm. Tony falls into a pool of his own blood, gasping for air as his gun lands on the floor. Megan fights her way out of Drew's grasp and runs over to him. Tears start falling from her eyes as she runs a hand through Tony's hair and holds his hand.

There is nothing she can do, Tony is dead.

The gun man who had shot Tony comes out from the shadows of the garage and stands with Drew. They nod to each other and then look back over to Megan. Drew and the other gun man remain stone faced, watching Megan urgently try to revive Tony.

"When you're done with him, why not come over here." Drew says with a laugh grabbing hold of his crotch, "I've got something for you to rub sweetheart."

Anger washes through Megan's face as she reaches out and grabs Tony's gun. She points the weapon towards Drew and the gun man and slowly raises it to protect herself. Drew and the gun man just watch her emotionlessly and unintimidated.

"What are you waiting for girl?" Drew asks coldly, "Kill us. Kill us both."

Megan's tears roll down her eyes and the gun shakes with her nervous hands. She keeps her eye locked onto Drew, her thoughts searching for a way out of this garage. Megan fires the gun, planting a bullet into Drew's shoulder. In surprise, Drew grabs his shoulder and yells out in pain.

"You fucking bitch." Drew screams, as the gun man lifts his weapon. Megan fires at the gun man, the bullet hitting his chest and bringing him down to the ground.

The blasts from the gunshots ring throughout the garage, catching the attention of several other thugs in the area. Megan hears them coming towards her, knowing that she can't fight them all. Megan places the safety on the gun and runs out of the garage at full speed. She is a very good distance away from the thugs, since they stop to help Drew up from the ground. Drew tells them what has happened and they pile into a car to chase Megan down. Two of the four thugs lift the gun man up from ground, trying to stop the intensive bleeding in his chest.

Megan runs into the rain, thinking only about going to safety and finding Amy as fast as possible. She knew this deal is a scam, why did she allow Amy to go through with it? Megan should have known better, she used to live and operate with mobsters in her past. Megan is more street smart than Amy is, she should have been able to convince Amy to not go through with this.

She runs faster, hearing the sound of a roaring engine. She looks behind her and the bright headlights of the black convertible shine upon her. The car is raging at full speed towards her, catching up to her very quickly.

Picking up speed, Megan runs faster, hoping that more cars will drive onto the road to divert the black convertible. Her prays are answered, and since Megan is running the opposite direction of traffic, the cars quickly turn the road into a huge obstacle course for the black convertible.

The black convertible narrowly dodges the other cars each time one gets in it's way. Megan can feel herself getting tired but she forces herself to pick up speed. The black convertible dodges the last of the cars on the street and picks up speed in its pursuit of Megan.

A narrow alley opens up in the corner and Megan runs into it. She still has a good lead over the black convertible, however, the car is gaining very fast. Megan runs through the long alley determined to get away. She notices a huge gate directly in front of her that cuts the alley in half. There is no way the black convertible can get past the gate. Megan takes a running start and leaps onto the gate, gripping the steel and pulling herself up as fast as she can.

Climb up the gate and get out. Simple.

Megan climbs up the gate at top speed as the black convertible rages into the alleyway. It is a very tight fit for the convertible; the side mirrors of the car are scratching against the wall of the alley. No matter what though, the convertible still rages forward. Megan can feel the anger from the men in the car bearing down on her as the car moves forward despite it's limited maneuverability. Megan reaches the top of the gate.

The black convertible slams hard into the gate, having no regard for its own wellbeing. The gate shakes violently and folds under the impact of the speeding car. Smoke comes out of the engine of the black convertible as it sits motionless underneath Megan.

Megan struggles to hold on, but the force of the hit makes her fall off the top of the gate. She lands on her back and shoulder on top of the vehicle. Megan flinches in pain as she feels half of her body go numb. Megan tries to roll off of the top of the car but her body refuses to cooperate.

The doors of the black convertible open slowly and three men walk out. Drew is one of them, holding his shoulder in pain. Seeing Megan helplessly laying out on the roof of the convertible makes Drew smile wider than he's smiled in a very long time. The other two thugs smile too, even though each one is still feeling the aftermath of the crash.

Megan's defeat is enough to heal all their wounds.

"Get her off the roof." Drew demands. The other two men eagerly do as they are told.

"No." Megan weakly screams, trying to fight back. Her body isn't responding to her pleas as the men pull her off the roof and hold her up to present her to Drew. Drew dominantly stands before Megan, staring mercilessly into her eyes.

"Let me go." Megan pleads as the two men handle her like a helpless rag doll. Despite his pain, Drew grabs Megan's chin and holds her face up to him.

"Cry you little bitch." Drew snickers, as Megan's tears fall from her eyes. It doesn't take Megan to long to realize that she is paralyzed on one side of her body. It also doesn't take her long to realize that she is at the mercy of Drew and the two thugs.

"Get the fuck off me." Megan screams at the men, refusing to give up her fight.

Drew violently punches her in the face. His shoulder buckles in pain because of the punch, but he doesn't mind it at all. The pain he is inflicting on Megan is enough to make him happy.

Drew forcefully grabs her by her hair and looks her directly in the eye. "I'm not going to kill you. You and I and the boys are going to have allot

of fun together back at the mansion. I promise."
Drew taunts.

The two thugs hold her firmly so that Drew
can kiss Megan on the lips. Megan tries to pull
away, but her body refuses to respond to her efforts.
Drew ends the kiss and licks his lips to savior the
taste of the kiss. The sound of another car engine
roars in front of the alley.

"Help." Megan screams as Drew and the
other two henchmen drag her towards the end of the
alley, "Someone please help me. Please."

A huge SUV pulls up to the opening of the
alley. The doors open and Drew enters the back
seat, followed by the two thugs who drag Megan
with them. They close the door of the SUV and
place Megan down right next to Drew. The driver
pulls a U turn to head back to Roman's mansion.

Megan doesn't have the physical capabilities
to try to fight back as she feels Drew's lips press
against hers and his hand crawl slowly up her thigh.

Unfortunately, he is rubbing the thigh that
she still has feeling in.

<C>   <E>   <O>

The damn locks were changed so she has to
pick the lock in order to enter Andy's shithole
apartment.

Vampyra performs the task easily and enters
Andy's apartment. How did he know that she has
the keys to his apartment? And where the hell did a
loser like him find the money to change the locks on
the door?

He better not have stolen her box and sold it
for money.

He wouldn't have the guts to do that.

So where the fuck is that box?

Vampyra searches the apartment up and down in order to find the small jewelry box she had given to Andy at Stalloni's Diner, and unfortunately, she doesn't find it anywhere.

Vampyra empties one of the drawers on the floor in frustration and places her hands on her hips. She never thought that it will be this hard to find a jewelry box that is misplaced in a small apartment like this one.

She walks over to the night table and starts to search those drawers when a knock on the door startles her. That can't be Andy, he would have keys to his own apartment. It can't be anyone else coming to the door because, let's face it, who will want to visit this place? Vampyra walks over the door, preparing herself to seduce who ever it is at the door.

Vampyra opens the door and smiles, seeing Amy standing in the doorway. Amy gasps at the sight of Vampyra. Vampyra grins, deciding to take advantage of her vulnerability. She places her hands on her hips and gives Amy a very sexy pose.

"Hey Amy." Vampyra playfully greets the woman, "Listen, if this isn't important, I'd really like to get back to fucking your boyfriend." Amy is speechless, and Vampyra smiles to show her enjoyment of the situation.

"I thought I was the only one who could do that?" a male voice says from behind Amy.

Vampyra watches Roman walk out from behind Amy. Roman grins at Vampyra, menacingly towering over Amy and enjoying the look of shock on Tessa's face.

Vampyra tries to slam the door closed, but Roman grabs the wooden door and flings it back at her. She stumbles onto the floor and Roman enters the apartment like a hyena searching for a fresh carcass. He ignores Amy, who slowly steps into the apartment to see if Andy is here. She is both saddened and relieved when she doesn't see him.

Roman grasps Tessa by the neck and lifts her off the ground, pressing her against the wall. Tessa tries to fight back, but Roman is too powerful for her. Roman grins evilly at her as he tightens his grip on Tessa's neck. He is strangling her very hard, and Amy watches the scene, extremely horrified of Roman's violent attitude.

"You think you can hide from me you tramp." Roman yells, strangling Tessa harder until her eyes start to tear, "I found you, you spoiled bitch."

Roman tosses Tessa to the floor. Tessa coughs and gags, trying to regain her breath as she attempts to rise up from the floor. Roman stomps away from her and walks around the apartment. Amy worriedly stares at Tessa, who is still trying to regain a normal breathing pattern.

Amy is frozen in fear, not knowing if she should help Vampyra or just leave her alone. She is too afraid to do either one, however, she is too scared of what will happen if she doesn't do anything. Amy has never seen anything more terrifying than Roman Castle, and she now realizes that she has just made a horrible mistake.

After searching the apartment and not finding Andy, Roman walks over to Amy. Roman stands in front of Amy, his eyes almost red with pure anger. "Where the fuck is Andy?" Roman yells at her. Amy looks up at him, horrified.

"You promised you wouldn't hurt him." Amy declares innocently.

"And you believed him." Tessa chokes out, finally being able to speak.

Roman moves away from Amy and back into Andy's living room. Roman kicks a few pieces of furniture and throws down several of Andy's belongings. "Stop destroying everything." Amy pleads weakly at Roman as he trashes random things in Andy's apartment. Amy runs over to Roman and grabs his arm as he lifts his fist to punch through the window. Roman turns over to Amy like a hawk and smiles widely as Amy's eyes widen with fear.

"You said that you wouldn't...." Amy pleads weakly.

Before she can say another word, Roman grabs Amy and slams her against the wall. Roman then grabs her by her neck and lifts Amy into the air. He strangles Amy as she grasps his hands, trying desperately to escape.

"Your boyfriend's not here Amy." Roman yells, "I don't like to be fucked with."

Out of the corner of his eyes, Roman sees Tessa getting up and trying to leave the room. Roman drops Amy and goes for Tessa, grabbing her hair and pulling her down to the ground. Tessa falls onto her back as Roman smiles, grabbing Tessa by her shirt and pulling her up to her feet.

"Where the fuck do you think you're going sugar?" Roman laughs, "You have something of mine, and it is in this apartment, isn't it?"

"It isn't here." Tessa declares, "Andy took it, he sold it and ran away with the money."

Roman smiles as he grabs Tessa's arm and twists it behind her back. Tessa winces in pain and Roman applied more pressure, taking pleasure out of Tessa's misery.

"You are lying to me Tessa." Roman growls, "We all know that Andy isn't capable of that." Roman pulls on Tessa's arm again, as Tessa fights against the pain and tears. "You know that you want to cry little girl." Roman snickers, "Now cry."

Tessa cries as Roman strengthens his grip on her. She is eventually brought down to her knees by Roman, who stares at her and smiles at Tessa's inability to fight him. Amy sees Tessa break down in front of her. Amy's entire body is frozen in fear as she watches the sight, trying to think how she can stop this form continuing.

Roman lets go of Tessa and throws her down to the floor. "Stay." Roman barks at her and Tessa does what she is told. Tessa tries desperately to stop crying and hide her pain, not wanting to show weakness in front of Roman Castle. Roman walks over to Amy and Amy can feel her muscles go limb and motionless. Roman stands before Amy, glaring at her with pure evil in his eyes.

"Where is Andy?" Roman yells at Amy once again.

"He's probably at work." Amy answers, "He should be home…."

"I don't have time to wait." Roman says, grabbing Amy by the arm and pulling her towards the doorway of the apartment.

"Let me go." Amy says, trying to fight back but Roman is too strong.

"Tessa come here." Roman orders as he pulls Amy out of the apartment. Tessa obeys Roman, following him out of the apartment like a loyal puppy. When they are all out of the room, Roman holds Amy in front of him and stares deep into his eyes.

"You didn't follow through with your deal."
Roman growls angrily.

"We can wait for him." Amy pleads "He is
probably coming home right now."

"I DON'T WAIT FOR ANYTHING."
Roman yells at Amy as Tessa stands behind them
with her head down like an obedient dog.

"What the hell is going on here?" Mr
McGuckin asks, wobbling out of his apartment in
shorts and a yellow T-shirt. The hair on his chest
has crumbs of potato chips in it and his breath is
stale and disgusting.

Roman and Amy look at Mr. McGuckin,
both surprised and disgusted by the sight of the
man. The three stare at each other in an awkward
silence, each one unsure of what to do. Tessa
remains behind Roman, unaffected by Mr.
McGuckin's presence. Mr. McGuckin smiles a
greasy grin as Roman eyes the disgusting Irish man,
waiting for him to involve himself in the situation.

"Are you one of those pimps who sells
whores?" Mr. McGuckin growls lustfully.

Roman smiles a weasel's grin and he glares
at Amy. Mr. McGuckin has his eyes on her. Amy
looks on in fear, feeling Roman tighten his grip on
her hands.

"It depends." Roman says, pointing at
Andy's apartment, "Do you know where the man
who lives in this apartment is?"

"Oh yeah." Mr.McGuckin says, "You're
talking about Andy aren't you?"

"Yes." Roman answers anxiously, "Do you
know where he is?"

"I do." Mr.McGuckin smirks, "And I'll tell
you if you are willing to give me one of your
whores for free."

Mr. McGuckin licks his lips as he eyes Amy. Roman gives Amy the evilest grin that she has ever seen, his grip on her strongly tightening around her hand.

"No." Amy desperately pleads, as Roman turns Amy towards Mr. McGuckin, "No, you can't do this." Amy desperately tries to fight out of Roman's grasp, but her efforts are to no avail.

Roman presents Amy in front of Mr. McGuckin, holding her arms behind her with one hand and her forehead with the other.

"You can kiss her and grope her, but that is it." Roman informs the fat greasy man, "Afterwards, if you don't tell me what I want to know, I will end your life." Mr. McGuckin nods in agreement, giving Roman a horny grin. Roman pushes Amy closer to Mr. McGuckin and she fights desperately in order to free herself.

Mr. McGuckin's dirty tongue licks his lips and he rubs his hands together in anticipation. He presses himself up against Amy, his mouth watering as he pulls his right hand into his crotch to rub his privates.

"No please don't do this." Amy begs.

Before Amy can finish her sentence, Mr. McGuckin's lips cling onto hers for a kiss. Amy's cries are muffled by his sticky and filthy tongue moving inside of her mouth. Mr. McGuckin continues to pleasure himself with his right hand as his left hand crawls onto Amy's waist and underneath her shirt. With his tongue still in Amy's mouth, Mr. McGuckin slides his hands along Amy's chest to fondle her breasts.

Mr. McGuckin pulls his lips off of Amy's and slides his tongue along her check and neck. Amy stops trying to fight back, her voice silenced by her tears and lose of dignity. She cries harder and more painfully as his lips kiss her collarbone and his hands reach through her bra and grabs a handful of her chest. He rolls her nipples between his fingers and orgasms into his hand, groaning in satisfaction. He brings his soiled right hand around her waist and pushes it into her pants. He starts rubbing her ass with his semen coated hand, getting hornier and hornier by the second.

Roman pulls Amy away from Mr. McGuckin after several minutes of allowed pleasure. He throws Amy to the ground, and she lands hard on her side, clutching herself to try and relieve her body of the humiliation she has just experienced. Roman quickly grabs the collar of Mr. McGuckin's shirt, who is still feeling the pleasure of his orgasm.

"Where is he?" Roman demands.

Mr. McGuckin turns his focus to Roman, quickly becoming serious at the sound of Roman's commanding voice. "I saw him run through the alley on the side of the building." Mr. McGuckin states, "It's a dead end, so he should be trapped there."

Roman lets go of Mr. McGuckin and storms towards the stairs. He grabs Amy and forcefully pulls her off the floor and into his arms. Amy weakly allows herself to be taken, not having the emotional or mental strength to fight him. Roman turns to Tessa to finally acknowledge her presence.

"Tessa." Roman orders, "Follow me."

Tessa obediently nods her head and follows Roman downstairs.

CHAPTER 9

Andy wakes up in the morning in the same shelter that he was invited to last night. The rain has stopped and the sun is shining brightly on his face.

He feels better waking up that morning, the warmth that the homeless family provided to him is something that he hadn't felt since the last time he was in Amy's arms.

He felt hope and closure.

And more importantly, he felt loved.

Andy's vision fully clears and he looks up into the sun. He blocks his eyes from the bright rays, wondering why it is shining so brightly through the wooden roof of the small shelter.

It didn't take him long to find out the reason why.

The roof of the small shelter isn't there.

As a matter of fact, the small wooden shelter isn't there at all.

Andy looks around in shock and horror as he sees destroyed pieces of wood surrounding the blankets and sheets that he has fallen asleep on. The entire structure has been destroyed and left to rot out in the middle of the alley.

Along with the family. The father, mother, son and daughter who took him in last night are all laid out on the floor all around him dead. They have all been shot in their sleep, and left to bleed to death in the blankets that kept them warm.

Andy looks around him at the wood and dead bodies, completely horrified and saddened by the massacre around him. How did he not realize what was going on? He can go to the police, but odds are several police officers have already walked

by and noticed the massacre and did absolutely
nothing.

He stands up, collecting the blankets in the
area in his hands and wrapping them around the
family. It isn't much, but they do deserve to have
some type of funeral. While wrapping the family,
Andy notices a letter addressed to him laying on the
floor. The envelope is stained with blood, and
Andy realizes instantly that this family died because
of his presence here. This realization only saddens
him even more.

Andy opens the envelope and reads the letter
that is inside.

*Meet me at 7 pm tonight at my home
at 79 Harold Square. Come alone and bring me my
jewelry box. Vampyra and Amy will die at exactly 7
pm if you are late. Take this note seriously.*

Roman Castle

Andy's face grows in terror. Roman Castle,
Vampyra mentioned him before. He is the man
who wants Vampyra dead. How did he find him?
How did Amy get involved? Is Amy okay? What
box is this man talking about?

Andy shakes his head in emotional
frustration at the questions that are brought up in his
mind. He places his hands inside of his pockets,
trying to think of a solution to his problems. The
fact that Vampyra is in danger doesn't phase him,
but having Amy in danger makes him more scared
than anyone will imagine. How did Roman even
know she existed? How is he going to get her...

The box.

His hand touches the small black box that Vampyra had given to him the first day that they met. He pulls the black box out of his pocket and examines it, not believing that such a small treasure caused as much problems as it has. What is this treasure that Vampyra and Roman seem to care about so much?

It doesn't matter. This black box is the only thing that can save Amy.

Andy will return it and hopefully, his life will return along with it.

It is too early to go down to Roman's mansion, but Andy doesn't care. He quickly checks his pockets, seeing if he can find anything that he can use as bus or train fare.

There is nothing.

Andy hangs his head in shame and pockets the small black box.

He begins the long walk to Roman's place.

<C>   <E>   <O>

When she returned to Roman's mansion last night, Amy was greeted by Roman's henchmen. They were carrying Tony's dead body outside to the dumpsters to be properly disposed of. Later, Amy witnessed Drew dragging Megan over to his private quarters. Megan is still alive, and she looks at Amy helplessly as Drew pulls her out of sight. Amy watched Megan until she was gone.

And then all she heard was Megan's screams......

Amy has been crying ever since she saw Roman destroy the wooden shack and kill the homeless family in their sleep with a silencer. Seeing Tony dead and hearing Megan's tortured screams all night long only make her continue to cry, and even harder than before.

And with all of that, there is the extremely humiliated and polluted feeling all over her body because of Mr. McGuckin's kissing and groping on her. The emotionally and physically traumatizing experience scars her even worse than when she was raped at her prom. She wants to hold herself for comfort, but the longer she does, the more dirty she feels. Amy begged Roman and his guards to allow her to shower, but no one heard or cared about her pleas.

All she was trying to do was help Andy...

"You can't help anyone in Windwill Town so stop crying about it." Tessa snaps at Amy as if she read Amy's thoughts.

It is nearing nightfall again and the room is getting dark. Tessa and Amy are locked in a room somewhere in the basement of Roman's mansion. Neither one slept all night, Amy because she couldn't stop crying and Tessa because Amy's crying kept her up.

Tessa is miserable sitting in the barely furnished and cold room with Amy. Having met Andy and now Amy, Tessa can see why the two of them were meant for each other. They are both honest, good natured people whose generosity and sincerity will eventually get them murdered in Windwill Town. Tessa pitied their lack of survival skills and grasp of the real world.

"Can you just stop already?" Vampyra snaps, "Your friends are dead and crying will not bring them back."

"This is my fault." Amy cries, not listening to Vampyra, "I should not have come here."

"You're absolutely right." Vampyra yells at her, "Anybody in town would have told you not to trust Roman Castle, you have to be a very naïve and idiotic person to have gotten yourself and your friends into this. I hope that everyone's death makes this experience worth something to you."

"I want Megan here with me." Amy continues, "Megan would know what to do. I should have listened to her."

"Your friend is dead." Vampyra snaps, in a matter of fact tone, "You will be too if we don't get out of here."

"I'm not listening to you." Amy snaps at Vampyra, "You are the one who hurt Andy. He didn't deserve this."

"I did what I had to do to survive." Vampyra explains, "Roman is trying to kill me and Andy offered his help."

"You made him help." Amy says.

"He offered to help." Vampyra replies, getting into Amy's face, "How childish are you? Forget about your friends and Andy, we will die in this house if we don't find a way out."

"He won't kill us." Amy innocently says, "He just wants the box back and he will let us go."

"God, you are an idiot." Vampyra sighs, completely annoyed, "You are just like Andy. You have no sense of the world around you and no survival skills what so ever. You and Andy are pathetic and useless people, which is why all of your friends are dead and you and Andy are going to join them."

Vampyra storms away from Amy, leaving her completely speechless and feeling even more upset than she already feels. Vampyra really can't take much more of Amy's crying, hoping that

Roman will kill her soon so that Tessa won't have to deal with her much longer.

"My dear Tessa." Roman says, "Why are you talking to this woman so harshly?"

Roman walks into the room, smiling as Amy and Tessa look up at him. Roman has a very sincere look on his face, the complete opposite of what he portrayed when he murdered the homeless family. Amy curls into a corner in the room, afraid of what Roman will do to them.

"She won't stop crying." Tessa snaps in frustration, "She should deal with the fact that she has made a huge mistake and move on."

"But she is scared Tessa." Roman replies softly, "And yelling at her will only make things worse." Roman looks over at Amy, who is still huddled into the corner in fright. He smiles warmly, trying to calm her down. Amy's fear keeps her from registering Roman's smile as being sincere.

"Are you okay my dear?" Roman asks politely.

"I want Megan here with me." Amy begs, "Please bring her here."

"I promise that we will release you and Megan the moment Andy comes with my jewelry box." Roman says to Amy, "That is if Megan isn't already dead."

More tears stream down Amy's eyes and Roman just watches her, unaffected by her sadness. Tessa sighs with frustration and to turns to Roman. She stands in front of him with an innocent smile.

"Come on Roman." Vampyra whispers, "I know you really don't want to kill me. I'm your little girl and the only woman you truly love."

"You're also a toy." Roman flatly adds, holding onto Vampyra's neck, "Whose legs I can spread open like a chicken wing." Roman lets her go slowly, and Vampyra still maintains her smile.

"And you love that about me too." Vampyra whispers softly, moving herself off of Roman and walking towards the wall. She turns back to Roman and bites her lower lip. Roman Castle just watches her unaffected by her seduction.

"The only way anyone will die tonight is if I don't get my box back." Roman tells Amy and Tessa, "And I suggest that you ladies freshen up. Our guest should be arriving shortly."

Without another word, Roman leaves the room, closing and locking the door behind him.

<C>   <E>   <O>

Andy finally reaches Roman's mansion. It is 6:45 pm.

Despite the breaks he was forced to take, Andy's body is sore and exhausted from having walked so long. However, he is able to find the strength to keep standing and moving. He has to save Amy, and moving forward is the only way to do so.

With no apartment to live in…

With no money to support him…

And with no job to aid him…..

Amy is the only thing in his life worth fighting for. Amy always stood by him and believed in him when no else would. She helped him and supported him emotionally, physically and mentally for so many years. He loves her more then anything in the world, and he can't allow her to get hurt because of his stupidity.

Why did he involve himself with Vampyra's life?

How did this women have the power to destroy his entire life in just a few days?

He didn't know who Vampyra was, and he doesn't fully understand why she is in trouble, or if she is in trouble to begin with, but he now no longer cares.

The only thing that matters now is Amy's survival.

His own survival is optional.

Andy walks up the stairs of Roman's mansion and to the front door. He knocks on the door. "Roman." Andy calls out as his fist pounds on the mansion door, "Roman." Andy's voice is hoarse from not having anything to eat or drink in hours. Nobody is answering the door. Amy has to be safe, he is early for the meeting…

SOMEONE OPEN THE GODDAMN DOOR!!!!!

The door opens instantly, and Andy falls into the mansion. The butler helps Andy to his feet and greets him with a very polite smile.

"Hello Andy, we have been expecting you." The butler says with sincere hospitality.

Andy gathers himself as the butler closes the door behind him. The butler guides Andy inside of the mansion and over to Roman's massive living room. He pulls out a seat for Andy to sit on and Andy happily takes it. Roman is already sitting there, cigar in hand and waiting patiently as the butler makes sure that Andy is comfortable.

"Would you like anything to drink Andy?" the butler asks, as Roman still sits and says nothing.

"No, I'm fine." Andy says completely exhausted.

"I insist upon giving you a glass of water sir." The butler says, "You must have had a long trip."

"Get him two glasses of water with ice." Roman orders politely, "He has had a hard day."

"Yes sir." The butler says, leaving to get the water.

When Andy is settled, he looks up at Roman, surprised by his hospitality. Roman places his cigar down in the ash tray and smiles at Andy his demeanor remaining polite and calm.

"I'm glad that you are here." Roman says, "I'm Roman Castle. Roman offers his hand in friendship, but Andy doesn't accept it. Roman retracts his hand.

"Where's Amy?" Andy asks, "Is she okay?"

"Amy is unharmed." Roman says, "And she will be released when you give me back what belongs to me."

"You can have it." Andy says, taking the box out of his pocket and holding it out to Roman.

"Why are you in such a rush?" Roman asks, not reaching for the box, "I wanted to talk to you man to man first."

"I don't want to talk." Andy answers in exhaustion, "I don't want anymore to do with this. Just please take the box and release Amy."

"And you don't care about what happens to Tessa?" Roman asks.

"No." Andy pleads, "I just want Amy to be safe. Just please take this box and release her."

"I'll take the box." Roman says, "But first, I want to know who you are, and why you decided to go against me in the first place."

"I'm nobody." Andy answers, "I am a nobody who tried to help someone out of a problem.

I am not a threat to you, and I am not a person who you should fear or respect. I just thought that, for once, I could make a difference in someone's life."

Roman remains silent, slowly nodding his head as he thinks over what has just been told to him. The butler places Andy's two glasses of water on the table right by him. Andy doesn't reach for them. Roman gestures for Andy to take the glasses and drink, but Andy still doesn't move.

"Come on Andy." Roman speaks politely, "Drink the water, I'm not going to poison you."

Andy drinks some water. He is really thirsty.

Andy drinks both glasses quickly, the cool taste of the liquid refreshing his body and making him feel more relaxed. Roman allows Andy a few seconds to savor these feelings before continuing to speak.

"You are wrong Andy." Roman says as Andy places the last glass down, "You are someone. You are one of the few people in Windwill Town who actually care about the lives of the people that walk the streets. You are a man who will not be bought, and who will not sell out to the highest bidder. You are a man who chooses true love in a woman instead of physical lust. You are a man who chooses to work responsibly for your survival instead of taking part in the town's regular activities. You are a selfless man, who will help the less fortunate even though you yourself are amongst them. You are one of the only genuinely good people left in Windwill Town, and for that, I want to show my respect to you."

Roman offers Andy his hand. Andy hesitantly shakes Roman's hand. Roman tightens his grip on Andy's hand, not allowing Andy to break the hand shake. The two men lock eyes and Roman begins to speak again. Suddenly, Roman's hospitality has faded and his face is now cold and emotionless.

"And because of who you are." Roman snickers, "You are also one of the most pathetic human beings living in this town, easily manipulated by the powerful individuals that live here. You are an innocent, desperate, helpless and obedient laborer who works in order to make the rich richer. If the town didn't have people like you to rob, manipulate and overwork, people like me wouldn't be as successful as we are."

Roman lets go of Andy's hand and takes his box, leaving Andy speechless and disgraced. Roman opens the box, taking out the jeweled ring that is inside of it. He places the ring on the finger that is without a ring, thus completing his ten ring set.

Andy stares at the ring, feeling even more stupid and pathetic then he felt before. He destroyed his life and put Amy's life in danger because of Roman Castle's stolen pinky ring. As Roman admires his completed set of rings, Andy can only think of how much everything he lost isn't worth the pinky ring that Roman is now admiring.

"I don't know why my little Tessa would steal from me. She doesn't appreciate all that I have done and sacrificed in order to make sure that she is safe." Roman says, as if he is thinking out loud. Roman stays silent for a moment and then turns to Andy and smiles.

"Tessa likes to play games with other peoples lives you see, and for that, she needs to be punished." Roman tells Andy. He pauses once again, taking a moment to collect himself.

"Someone will die by my hands tonight." Roman decides.

"But you said you weren't going to kill anyone." Andy replies with terror in his eyes.

"People can say anything, but their actions always speak otherwise." Roman states.

Roman stands and heads towards the door. "Tessa and Amy are outside waiting for you." Roman says, "I will lead you there."

Andy follows Roman outside. Neither man says a word to each other as they walk through the hallway and leave the mansion. Andy stares at Roman, wondering what is about to happen and what he can actually do to save Amy. Roman simply looks onward, walking with murderous intent towards the front door.

Roman opens the door and allows Andy to walk outside first. Tessa and Amy are in front of them, held hostage by Roman's guards. Amy is crying and trying desperately to fight them off while Tessa allows herself to be held. Tessa doesn't let her guard down though as she waits patiently for the opportunity to escape.

Amy and Andy lock eyes as soon as Andy walks outside of the mansion. Amy stops crying as Andy gazes at her, feeling a wave of happiness inside his body because she is still alive.

"Amy." Andy calls out, heading for her as another one of Roman's guards grab him and hold him back.

"Andy help me." Amy screams as she tries to fight the guards. Tessa laughs at the hopelessly romantic sight before her. Roman simply stands between all three of his victims and watches the sight around him.

"Calm down, everyone will get what they want shortly." Roman announces. Roman digs into his pocket and pulls out a gun. Andy stops fighting the guards, freezing in terror when he notices Roman cocking his gun.

"Someone will die tonight Andy" Roman states while walking towards Amy and Tessa, "And it is up to you to choose who it will be."

"You got your ring back don't kill anyone." Andy pleads and Roman laughs.

"If only it was that simple." Roman says, lifting the barrel of the gun towards Andy, "Now choose, or I'll kill you."

"Please don't hurt him." Amy begs.

"I won't unless he tells me to." Roman informs her.

Andy watches everyone with terror in his eyes. Roman maintains his position, holding the gun to Andy's face and growing more impatient with every moment that passes. Amy is desperately trying to free herself, while Tessa watches the sight without any fear. Andy doesn't want anyone to die, there is no reason to kill anyone over a stupid pinky ring. As the seconds tick away, he tries to figure out how to save everyone's life.

"I don't want to kill anyone." Andy pleads, "It isn't worth it."

"Then kill yourself." Roman replies, in a matter of fact tone, "Your decision to help Tessa is one of the reasons why this has happened."

"Just let us all go." Andy insists

Roman pulls the gun back, impatient and frustrated by Andy's lack of cooperation. "Alright fine then I will choose for you." Roman says.

Roman turns to the two women, looking back and forth between the two of them. Amy's fright increases. Tessa is smiling at Roman now, looking him deep in the eyes. Roman smiles back at her and she licks her lips seductively towards him. They make a connection that is deeper than just looking into each other's eyes. Roman can feel his very soul reaching out to Tessa, truly proud to see his little Tessa in his life once again.

"Release Amy and allow her to go with her boyfriend." Roman commands his guards without hesitation, "Tessa will die today."

"What?" Tessa exclaims as the guards let Amy go.

Andy is released as well and Amy runs into his arms. Andy hugs her firmly and romantically and she returns the hug, happy to finally be able to hold him and see that he is okay.

"I missed you. I was so afraid you were dead." Amy declares happily, as she holds him warmly in her arms.

"I'll never allow anything to happen to you." Andy says, "I'm sorry I haven't been there for you. You and Megan and Tony are all I have and I'm sorry that..."

Amy lets go of Andy and looks into his eyes while holding his hands. "Megan and Tony are dead." Amy sadly tells him. Andy stares at Amy, as more waves of sadness wash through his face.

"How?" Andy asks, "How did they..."

"It's my fault." Amy explains, "They warned me. They told me not to come here and now they are dead." Amy starts to cry and Andy holds her in his arms to comfort her.

"What the hell are you doing?" Tessa asks as the guards throw her into Roman's arms. Roman holds her firmly, keeping her from escaping as he presses the barrel of the gun against Tessa's waist.

"You have always been an ungrateful whore." Roman mocks, as Tessa desperately tries to escape, "I did everything for you and you never appreciated any of it."

"You know me." Tessa pleads in terror, "Andy and Amy are nothing to you. They don't have the history that we have."

"That only makes your death more fulfilling." Roman replies coldly, "Murdering you will give me tremendous satisfaction."

"And keeping me alive will satisfy you in other ways." Tessa adds.

Tessa kisses Roman passionately and he returns the kiss. She slips her tongue into his mouth and he goes along with her kiss willingly. Suddenly, he grabs her by the hair and pulls her head back. She let's out a painful scream as Roman looks down into her eyes threateningly.

"All whores go to hell." Roman snarls as he brings his gun to Tessa's face. Tessa looks into his eyes and sees a purely murderous stare. He holds her like a boa constrictor and Tessa can feel pure fear running through her veins. Roman's grip is too strong for her to escape as he slides the gun lustfully along her sternum.

"Time to die sweetheart." Roman whispers to Tessa.

Andy and Amy pay no attention to what is happening around them. They have each other now and that is all that matters to either of them. Andy and Amy start to walk away from the scene, both of them trying to figure out what they will do in the future. None of Roman's guards stop them since nobody thinks that Andy and Amy's presence matter anymore.

Roman's finger squeezes the trigger. Tessa hears the trigger pulling back and she closes her eyes, praying that despite all her sins, she will be allowed to go to heaven. Time slows for a moment, as Tessa can hear every sound that the bullet makes as it fires out of Roman's gun.

A gunshot riddles through the air as Tessa's body goes into shock in Roman's arms. Roman looks down into her beautiful eyes and perfectly clear face, admiring her unmatchable beauty and features. Tessa looks up at Roman's cold stare, searching for some type of compassion within his soul. She finds nothing, and Roman casually pushes Tessa's body down to the ground.

Surprisingly, Tessa is able to catch herself before she hits the ground. She quickly checks herself for a wound and realizes that she has not been shot. Tessa looks up at Roman in confusion. He meets her gaze and then turns over to where Andy and Amy are.

Andy is holding Amy in his arms when she suddenly collapses inside of them. Andy looks at her in alarm, and her whole body slumps over, causing him to stumble forward. Amy can no longer hold herself up and she collapses onto the pavement, bringing Andy down with her.

"No, no." Andy screams, noticing the bullet wound in Amy's back. He grabs Amy and turns her around, looking into her eyes as she breathes in deeply in order to gain as much air as possible. Amy chokes in pain and agony as Andy cries and holds her.

Tessa turns back to Roman in relief and is shocked to find the barrel of the gun once again pointed at her.

"Get up." Roman orders and Tessa obeys. There is an awkward silence now, the two destined lovers looking into each other's eyes waiting for the next move.

"I would never hurt you my dear." Roman tells her, "I love you too much to see you die."

"I knew you wouldn't kill me." Tessa replies, "You would never forgive yourself."

"My offer to you still stands." Roman states, "I will pay for you to live and survive in this town. You can and will have everything that you want, as long as you never show yourself around me or my home or anyone connected to me ever again."

Roman moves closer to her so that his shadow completely engulfs her. He shows his dominance over her in his gaze and she looks deep into his eyes.

"If you don't agree to this." Roman says, "Or if you ever choose to cross me again, I will see to it that your life is a living hell."

Tessa looks deep into Roman's eyes, searching for the compassion in him that she missed so much. She can tell that he is looking deep inside of her as well, searching to see if the innocent young Tessa that he had raised is still inside the seductress that stands before her.

"I took the ring because I miss you." Tessa admits with genuine child-like innocence shining in her eyes, "I wanted to have you close to me at all times."

Roman looks deep into her eyes and takes her by the hand. He opens her hand and places the same pinky ring that she had stolen into her palms. He closes her hand and gives her a warm paternal smile

"All you had to do was ask." Roman says softly, as Tessa smiles and holds the ring against her heart.

Tessa kisses her finger tips and presses it against Roman's lips. He accepts the kiss and she looks deep into his eyes. "I wish I could find someone who will love me as purely as you do." Tessa says, allowing what is left of her insecurity and innocence to show in her voice.

"Feelings are mutual." Roman says, softly and compassionately. Roman waves his hands, motioning for all of his men to return to the mansion. The men obey his orders and file out of the front lawn. Tessa watches Roman go and he watches her as well, wanting to hold onto every second that Roman is in her sight.

Andy holds Amy in his arms as he sits down on the pavement. She desperately tries to breath in more air as she looks up into the eyes of the man she loves.

"Please don't leave." Andy pleads to the guards around him, "I need an ambulance for her. Please, call me an ambulance."

Roman and his men shut the door without another word or even a look in Andy's direction. Tessa watches the door, wishing that Roman will come back outside and allow her back into his life.

She knows it isn't going to happen, and for the sake of both of them, it is better that way.

Andy looks down into Amy's eyes. "I...love you." Amy gasps weakly as she runs a hand onto Andy's face. Andy can feel her blood running onto his hands and face. Andy holds her, his mind racing trying to figure out what to do in order keep her alive. Amy is the only person that ever made his life mean anything, he can't possibly go on without her.

"Please don't die." Andy begs, clutching Amy, "I need you to survive. You don't deserve this."

Vampyra walks past Andy, putting her cell phone away after calling herself a cab. Andy looks up at Vampyra as she walks past him to go to the end of the road. Vampyra doesn't even take the time to notice that he and Amy are there.

"Please I need your phone to call the police." Andy cries to Tessa, grabbing hold of her ankle. Tessa stops, suddenly looking down at Andy and wondering why he has just touched her. She kicks his hand off of her ankle and rolls her eyes at Andy.

"Please." Andy begs, "I need help."

"And waste my cell phone minutes on her." Vampyra snaps, "Listen, my cab is coming in few minutes. I don't have time for this."

"But I helped you." Andy begs clutching onto Amy's body, "She is going to die if...."

"She is going to die anyway." Vampyra replies completely annoyed, "You think the police are going to come all the way down here for her? This is Roman Castle's mansion, the police don't come here."

"They will come." Andy replies with hope, "Please let me use your phone."

Vampyra rolls her eyes and checks the time on her watch. She looks down at Andy and shakes her head. "Listen, I'm going to tell you one last time." Vampyra says, "This is Windwill Town, honey. People die everyday. If she isn't going to die today, then there will be a good chance that she will die tomorrow. No cop in the world can prevent that from happening."

"She is all I have left." Andy begs in tears.

Vampyra sighs and kneels down next to Andy and takes hold of his hand. She places Roman's pistol in his hands and smiles. She closes his hand around the handle of the gun and she runs a hand through his hair. Andy looks at her in sad confusion, wondering why she isn't helping him.

"You're a sweet guy, so I'm going to give you some advice." Vampyra says as politely as she possibly can, "There is one more bullet left in this gun. Do yourself a favor and join her."

A cab pulls up to the road and honks it's horn to catch Vampyra's attention. Vampyra stands up and walks away from Andy, not turning back or hesitating even once. She catches her cab and steps inside, telling the driver where her apartment is.

Andy desperately calls out to Vampyra, begging her to come back. It doesn't take long for Andy to realize that she is ignoring him. The cab drives away from Vampyra, and just like that, Andy and Amy's existence in this world no longer matter.

Andy looks back into Amy's face. She is no longer breathing and her eyes are motionless and locked in on his. Andy holds her, feeling her cold blood run through his hands and along his arms.

"Amy." Andy calls out to her in a soft whisper, hoping to have her wake up in his arms, "Amy please wake up." Amy doesn't move or respond. She just stares at Andy with a motionless and glassy look in her eyes.

Andy cries hard while he holds the woman that he loves. Nothing in his life has ever been more important to him than Amy. She always thought of him as something when the whole world saw him as nothing.

And now she is dead. Because of his mistake to try to help someone in Windwill Town, Amy, an innocent person in this situation, is dead. Amy never hurt anyone and didn't do anything to deserve the fate that beheld her. All she wanted to do was save the man she loved.

Worse than that, Tony and Megan are also dead. Three people who had nothing to do with the situation are all dead because of Andy's mistake to try and help the wrong person.

He thought that for once in his life, he can make a difference in someone's life. But he didn't think that that difference would be the end of the lives of three innocent people who he held most dear to his heart. Andy now realizes that his life did mean something because he had Amy, Tony and Megan by his side. He is a good boyfriend and a good friend, and that is enough to make him someone special.

Why couldn't he have seen this sooner?

Andy holds the gun in his hands, as his tears fall onto Amy's body. Vampyra is right, in Windwill Town, people die everyday. One more body doesn't make a difference, no matter who it is.

Andy places the barrel of the gun in his mouth and closes his eyes. Memories of his time with Amy, as well as the moments he had spent with Megan and Tony run through his mind as his tears fall onto the sidewalk. He looks up into the heavens, praying for forgiveness for what he has done to his friends.

A gunshot sounds through the night sky and everything is still once again.

EPILOGUE

This is the place known as Windwill Town, USA. A place where there is very little dreams for a safe future. A place that is run by anything and everything that is illegal or just plain screwed up. A place that is fueled by the pain and suffering of the kindhearted and caring souls of the neighborhood.

When one asks me what life is like in Windwill Town, some of the words that come to my mind are dangerous, deceiving, seductive and illegal. There are plenty more that I can tell you, but I believe that you have gotten the point after reading this story.

Windwill Town is more than just a town, it is an experience. Windwill Town is an entity that you must envision in order to understand. However, in order to do this, you may have to enter a place in your mind that you thought could never exist.

The lives and events of the people within this town are available and ready for you to witness, and I'm inviting you to sit down and make your own judgments on what you read. Whether you like what you read, or are disturbed by what lies before you, you will son understand what it is like to live in Windwill Town.

I invite you to the judge.

Welcome to Windwill Town, USA.

IF YOU ENJOYED THIS

WINDWILL TOWN BOOK,

MAKE SURE TO
LOOK OUT FOR

THE REST OF
THE SERIES.

CURRENTLY AVAILBLE
IS

BOOK #6
THE STRANGER

HERE IS A SNEAK PEAK:

Joe Colletti drives his car past the border of Windwill Town. He has never been to this place before and he probably wouldn't even have known where he was if the NOW ENTERING WINDWILL TOWN sign didn't give it away.

Colletti has been driving for hours on a road trip that seemed like it is taking him forever to complete. He is representing his precinct at a Police Officer Summit on the outskirts of Connecticut. At this summit, there will be a discussion on various new additions to the Police Code of Laws in the United States.

Joe Colletti is a high ranking homicide detective in Brooklyn, New York. Colletti has brought down the biggest, baddest and most dangerous criminals in one of the biggest cities in the United States. He is a rough and stern street fighter who always catches his man, even if he has to go above and beyond the rule book to do it. Colletti is a man with an attitude and a name that carries through New York's crime rings like a plague.

Anyone who knows the name Colletti, fears it.

In his personal life, Colletti is a proud and good father to his daughter Brenda. He and his wife, Angela, have a relationship that is on rocky ground, but that is a story entirely for another time.

He has to drive through Windwill Town in order to get through to Connecticut.

He shouldn't have even needed to though, but the main highway that leads thru the town has been closed for the night. What did the officer at the blockade tell him the reason was again? Something about illegal trafficking of some sort? Colletti can't remember, probably because he is too tired to even listen to the guy's answer. All Colletti really cares about is that the drive to Connecticut is now going to take longer since he has to use back roads in a town that he doesn't know anything about.

Colletti looks around the town and sees that the streets look pretty empty and dark. Where Colletti comes from, that usually means that the streets are crawling with muggers and murderers. Since this town looks so dead and the streets so cluttered with garbage, Colletti doesn't really think that there is anything going on around here.

Another few miles of driving and Colletti can feel himself falling asleep at the wheel. He looks around for a motel or something and all he sees are strip clubs and bars. He also sees several houses and apartment buildings in the area, none of which look to be as well maintained as the strip clubs and bars. But no motels as far as his sleepy eyes can see.

Colletti drives for another five minutes until he eventually finds a motel. It doesn't look like anything special, one can say that the building is decently maintained and it looks better than most of the houses he has seen. At the same time though, the area isn't that inviting. There is a lot of graffiti art covering the neighboring walls, implying that there are street gangs somewhere in the area.

However, it is close to the highway, and as long as there is a bed to sleep in and a warm cup of coffee waiting for him in the morning, why not just stay here for just one night.

Also, he doesn't think he can last another few minutes worth of driving.

Colletti pulls up to the Easton Motel between Bruer Street and Johnston Avenue. He parks his car in the parking lot and walks over to the motel's office. He enters the office, eager to get a room and sleep. In the morning, he can hop onto the highway and get back to his journey.

The motel's manager is sitting behind the large desk with his feet up and a newspaper in his hands. Colletti can't see his face through the newspaper and he isn't even sure that the man realizes that Colletti is there.

Or maybe he just doesn't care.

The office is clean. There is a line of keys on the wall next to the manager, meaning that the very little of the rooms in the motel aren't occupied. The trash is filled to the top and overflowing, which shows that the manager is just throwing out his garbage and not emptying it. The wallpaper in the office is peeling a little and the carpet feels old and worn out.

At the least, it is clean.

Colletti walks over to the desk and it still seems like the manager doesn't even realize that Colletti is in the room.

"Excuse me." Colletti says.

The man doesn't answer.

"Excuse me." Colletti repeats, his voice a little more stern.

The man doesn't answer.

"Hello, excuse me." Colletti says again.

Colletti hears a grunt from behind the newspaper.

"Can I have a room for the night please?" Colletti asks.

"Paper or plastic." The man behind the newspaper asks.

"Plastic." Colletti says.

"Machine is broken." The man replies.

"Paper." Colletti says.

There is a pause from behind the newspaper. "25 dollars." The man says.

Colletti places $25 on the desk and the man pulls it away from him just as quickly. As the hand with the money moves behind the paper another hand reaches for a set of keys and throws it at Colletti. Colletti catches it.

"Room 26." The man says.

Colletti looks at the keys. The number on the keys is 14.

"Pleasure doing business with ya." Colletti says, walking out of the office.

The whole time, the man doesn't even look up from his newspaper.

<C>   <E>   <O>

Colletti walks out of the office and enters Room 14. Room 14 looks just as nice as the office, except in this room, the trash can isn't overflowing. The TV's antenna is covered in aluminum foil and the bed sheets are faded. Allot of the furniture looks old and in need of replacing, just like the very bland and worn out carpeting.

What the hell kind of place is this? Don't they ever look after their stuff?

He walks on the carpet towards the bathroom. He inspects the bathroom to make sure that it is sanitary and luckily he discovers that it is. Colletti takes a leak and then washes his face with the soap. He walks over to the bed and also inspects that to see if it is clean. He lets out another sigh of relief when he discovers that the bed is indeed clean.

Colletti lays down on the bed and turns out the light, ready to sleep so that he can wake up early in the morning and head for Connecticut. Colletti closes his eyes and prepares to sleep.

Time for some shut eye.

A woman screams outside, opening Colletti's eyes only seconds after he had closed them. The woman screams for help once again as Colletti listens more intently. He hears the voices of two men laughing and mocking the woman. He can hear the woman being dragged past his room along the sidewalk outside of the motel. Her screams start to muffle and Colletti assumes that someone probably put a hand over her mouth. He hears one of the men scream out in pain and then a loud slap. Suddenly, Colletti can no longer hear the woman scream.

Colletti listens more and hears the door to one the rooms open and close. Isn't anyone going to do something? Aren't there any security guards in this place? Well, there were allot of keys in the office, so maybe he and those men are the only occupants.

But why would the manager give motel keys to two men dragging a woman around with them against her will?

He probably didn't look up from his paper.

Colletti gets out of his bed and steps out of his room. Colletti is tired, he can barely keep his eyes open and his body is exhausted. However, he can't just sit back and allow a woman to get killed or murdered in a motel room that is right next to his. Even without a badge, Colletti will come to her aid. So why should being outside of his jurisdiction stop him?

They can't be too far away.

Colletti quietly walks along the side walk, pressing his ear against the doors and listening for any type of sound. He walks up to Room 18 and hears the eager laughter of the same two men that he had heard earlier. He can't hear the woman anymore, which means that she is still out cold. There are probably two punk kids in the room trying to rape a young woman.

This shouldn't take long.

Colletti takes a few steps away from the door and then kicks it down. The two men in the room look up at Colletti, completely startled by his presence. One of them, a man in his late twenties with long hair and rough brown eyes is tying the woman's wrists to the bed post. The other man, in his thirties with a short scruffy beard, is sitting on top of the young woman in his underwear. He has his hands underneath her shirt probably, gripping her breasts firmly in his grasp. The woman looks 18 years old, a pretty young brunette with a good body and clear complexion. She is still out cold and there is bruise on the left side of her face.

"I'm trying to get some fucking sleep." Colletti says as the two men just stare at him in awe.

"Then do it asshole and leave us alone." Scruffy Beard says, holding the woman's breasts tighter, "We're busy."

"Looks to me like you're boring that girl." Colletti remarks, "You two can't satisfy a woman?"

Brown Eyes stands up and walks over to Colletti, getting into his face to challenge him. "How about minding your fucking business asshole?" the man growls at Colletti.

"Call me an asshole again and I'll shove something up yours." Colletti warns.

"Asshole." Brown Eyes taunts, staring deep into Colletti's eyes. Colletti smiles.

This shouldn't take long.

Colletti head butts Brown Eyes, breaking the man's nose in the process. Colletti punches the man in the stomach and then in the face as Scruffy Beard jumps off the young girl and reaches for his pants. Before the man can get his pants on, Colletti kicks Scruffy Beard in the ass and slams him into the wall. Scruffy Beard stumbles back into Colletti and is punched in the face. Scruffy Beard goes down.

Colletti moves over to the girl as Scruffy Beard painfully grabs his clothes. Brown Eyes gets up too, holding his nose up as the blood flows all over his hands. Scruffy Beard and Brown Eyes scurry out of the room quickly as Colletti lets out a laugh. He watches the two men run out into the night, laughing even harder when Scruffy Beard trips while trying to get his pants on.

Colletti looks over to the bed and sees the young woman laying there, still tied to the bed and unconscious. Scruffy Beard had tried to remove her clothes, so Colletti straightens her up. He unties her and lifts her into his arms.

He can't just leave her here, and she is still unconscious, so he can't take her home. He has to keep her safe until she wakes up.

He carries her to his room, noticing that nobody is around to try to figure out what has happened. Surely, someone, even the manager, must have heard the fight. Colletti walks over to his room and closes the door, locking it carefully just in case the guys come back.

He places the girl on the bed, resting her head on the pillow to keep her comfortable. There is no ice anywhere, so Colletti soaks a towel with cold water and places it on her forehead. Colletti places the covers over her body and checks once again to make sure she is comfortable.

Alright, time to go to bed.

Colletti looks at the bed and realizes that he can't sleep there with the girl in it. There isn't a couch anywhere and to top it off, there are no more blankets. "Shit." Colletti mumbles, "Can't a guy get some sleep?"

There is a chair near the bed pointing to the television. It is an old wooden chair with ragged cushions which doesn't look that sturdy. Colletti sits on it slowly to test out its strength.

It will hold him.

The chair isn't comfortable but it will have to do for tonight. Tomorrow morning he'll take the girl home and drive over to Connecticut and get the hell out of this place. Colletti closes his eyes and tries to go to sleep, making sure to keep one eye alert just in case the guys try to come back for the girl.

The manager in the office is most likely still reading the paper.

<u>OTHER TITLES COMING SOON</u>

BOOK 2 = THE MUTE

BOOK 3 = THE VIGILANTE

BOOK 4 = THE EXCHANGE

BOOK 5 = THE RULES

BOOK 7 = THE AMAZON

<u>FOR MORE INFORMATION ON</u>
<u>WINDWILL TOWN</u>
<u>GO TO</u>

<u>WWW.WINDWILLTOWN.COM</u>